Sherpa's Adventure

Saving The Future

Lori Costew

ISBN: 1481103911

ISBN 13: 9781481103916

Library of Congress Control Number: 2012922627
CreateSpace Independent Publishing Platform
North Charleston, South Carolina

Dedication

To every kid who made the right decision when it was really hard—keep being strong and smart because
YOU MAKE A DIFFERENCE!

Author's Acknowledgements

Not only does it take a village to raise children, but it also takes one to write a book. I am blessed to have the support of incredible family and friends. Much gratitude to Michele, Dawn and Gale for being my cheerleaders and early editors- you keep me positive! Big thanks to my test readers, including Amy and Sydney, whose ideas and feedback made this book much better. And to the lights of my life—Jeff, Troy and Cate—thank you for encouraging "Book Time" and being my constant source of inspiration. I love you!

Table of Contents

Chapter 1

Sherpa

"THREE WORDS: BEST. PARTY. EVER. MY Sweet Sixteen had to be the best night of my entire life!" Sherpa gushed into the Diary app on her communicator. "Friends from all over the Western World came that I haven't seen in forever. Mom had all my favorite munchies, and I ate so much! Good thing she ordered a hovering dance floor off the balcony, or I may have ended up in a food coma. It was wild to look down through the glass bottom. It made me a little dizzy in the beginning, but it was so cool to look up! There were a million stars in the sky, and it felt as if we were dancing right in the middle of the Little Dipper constellation. The music totally rocked! I'm not exactly the world's greatest dancer, but neither is Amy, and we didn't care how goofy we looked. I can't wait for her to come over later so we can talk about the party!"

Sherpa and Amy had been BFFs since they were practically babies and did EVERYTHING together. Amy couldn't care less that Sherpa was "first kid" and Sherpa's mom was the Ruler of the Western World—one of the two most powerful people on earth. The girls always had each other's backs.

Sherpa was standing at the window of the penthouse apartment suite she shared with her mother, Lillian, on the top floor of a two-hundred-story building. Since all buildings generated their own power through natural sources, there were no wires or poles getting in the way of the apartment's magnificent view—the ocean to one side and the mountains to the other. Similar to most homes in the year 2310, bursts of bright accent colors added style and texture to the primarily silver-and-gray interior. The furniture was comfortable, yet simple and streamlined. All the lights and appliances were "intelligent," having no cords or switches; they simply turned on and off when required. Rooms always looked organized because clutter was hidden behind movable drawers and cabinets; plus, the robots were always cleaning. Looking at the tidy apartment, Sherpa thought that one would never know a surprise party with over a hundred people had ended just several hours before!

Sherpa felt a touch on her shoulder. She bent down and gave her mom a huge bear hug. "Thank you for the incredible party! It was even better than the 2306 bash celebrating the End of all Wars. I don't know how you pulled it off. I was totally gobsmacked!"

Lillian grinned smugly. It was hard to get one over on Sherpa, who tended to make everyone's business her business. "What was your favorite moment?"

"Ohmigosh, how do I pick only one? Hmmm, I think it had to be toward the end of the party when I looked around and realized how lucky I am to have such amazing friends." Grinning impishly she added, "But the twelve-foot chocolate waterfall does come in a close second. I could have stood underneath it all night with my mouth wide open!" The two, still wearing their PJs, had just sunk into a comfy couch when a robot delivered steaming mugs of hot chocolate. "I just wish Dad could have been there."

Lillian's eyes glistened. "I know. I miss Bernard too. So much..."

The two sat in silence for a few moments sipping their hot chocolates before Sherpa asked, "Mom, why do you always change the subject when I want to talk about my becoming the chancellor of positivity? I'm ready to go!"

Sherpa REALLY wanted to be chancellor of positivity. She wanted it way more than anything in her entire life. The position was a full member of the Government Cabinet, and only a kid could hold it. It would be awesome to be in charge of something and make big decisions that affected kids throughout the Western World. She would travel to the coolest places!

Lillian cleared her throat. "Sweetheart, I do not want to ruin this great afterglow from the party, but I have to tell you that there is no impending appointment to that position."

Sherpa sucked in her breath, feeling as if a door had just been slammed in her face. "What! You always disagree with me! I've been preparing for years to be chancellor of positivity! Why won't you just officially declare my appointment and let me get started? After all, I worked my butt off in school to take academy and university classes so I could graduate early."

"Sherpa, you are very smart, and I'm so proud of your academic success. As Ruler of the Western World, I do have the ability to appoint you as chancellor of positivity. Even though the chancellor of positivity is the youngest member of the Cabinet, it is THE most critical position; it ensures that all kids' voices are heard! That position is responsible for the future of the Western World. As your mother, I want nothing more than to see you happy. But as ruler, it is my responsibility to take a broader view of this situation. I would rather the position stay empty for now. Someday you will be ready, but you have much to learn. You don't know what you don't know yet."

Sherpa rolled her eyes. "What the heck does that mean? Mom, everyone knows I'm the daughter of Lillian. Of course they will listen to me."

"Do you really think that you could be truly effective by simply walking in my shadow or using my power to control others?" When Sherpa didn't respond, Lillian continued. "People must respect you for your own knowledge and wisdom. You may not believe this, but I have been preparing you for this type of responsibility since the day you were born sixteen years ago. It is time for you to know the meaning behind your name because your dad and I chose Sherpa for a reason. As you know, Mount Everest is the largest mountain on earth. In this century, we can easily fly up to experience the exhilaration of standing at the top of the world. But hundreds of years ago, climbing to the summit required extensive physical preparation, proper equipment, and skilled guidance. In fact, a lot of people died trying to reach the top. We named you Sherpa after the men and women who guided climbers. The Sherpas played a critical role in the journey but provided support behind the scenes. They were smart, strong, and wise to the ways of the mountain."

"Wow, and here I always liked it because no other kids in my class had the same name. So your expectation of the chancellor of positivity is to guide people into having positive lives?"

"Good connecting the dots! The answer is yes and no. Even with all our twenty-fourth-century technology, we cannot force positive thinking or good decisions, or require people to be happy."

"Uh, Mom, that was really deep, and I didn't get much sleep last night. Please translate!"

Lillian thought for a moment. "OK, I think an example will make my point more clear. Remember your first year at the academy?"

"No!" moaned Sherpa, covering her reddening cheeks with her hands. "I wish I had a memory eraser for that entire period!" Sherpa had been a total idiot during the first couple weeks of school and didn't exactly make a positive first impression. She turned off all the kids by trying to act sophisticated and being something that she wasn't—a major bad decision on her part. It took the rest of the year to show everyone that she really wasn't a snob. "I'm so glad that Amy stayed my friend after that!" she said. "Just please don't say I told you so…" Eager to change the subject, Sherpa continued, "I think I get your point. The more people stay focused on making good decisions and choosing to be happy, the more likely they will have a positive life."

"Exactly—and sometimes it just takes one person to start a change that touches the entire planet. Believe it or not, I do have a purpose for this conversation and a better explanation regarding why I'm not ready to appoint you chancellor of positivity…for now. I've had Western World scientists working on a top secret project," Lillian said with a hint of mystery in her voice. "Get dressed. We are heading to the Technology Laboratory."

Thirty minutes later they entered the transport at the penthouse balcony and within moments were in flight headed toward the mountains. Lillian, as usual, was busy talking to someone on her communicator. The flight would take only about fifteen minutes. This was unusual; over the past four years, Lillian had taken Sherpa practically everywhere in the Western World, but Sherpa had never even heard of the Technology Laboratory.

She settled back into the comfortable chair for the ride. One of the advantages of being the daughter of the Ruler of the Western World was having access to the coolest transports. The latest transport was absolutely quiet—despite being the fastest transport on the planet, there was no engine noise or wind noise. Heck, the door didn't even make a sound when it closed. Sherpa wondered if it was this silent for the eagle she happened to notice soaring outside the window. Her favorite transport was one that doubled as a plane and a deep-water submarine. Last year, she and her mom had to visit a community that was constructed two miles under the surface of the ocean at the far end of the Western World. It was so amazing to go from watching seagulls to observing colorful fish and dolphins in matter of seconds.

Whenever Sherpa needed to travel within a couple thousand miles of the capital, she used the automatic pilot feature on the transport. She simply belted in and spoke the intended location into the GPS, and the transport took off. However, when she traveled with her mom, the security detail required a live pilot. While the first kid may be expendable to a malfunctioning automatic pilot, Lillian most certainly was not. Periodically after her mother had been dropped off for some meeting or another, Sherpa could sweet talk her way into a flying lesson. One of the pilots, Captain Gabe, had a niece Sherpa's age and could understand her need for speed. There was nothing more exciting than zooming to the edge of space. She was never allowed to cross that barrier, but she pushed it as far as she could. It was incredible to hover the transport right on the border between blue sky and black outer space. The stars were close enough to touch!

Sherpa's attention quickly turned away from the sereneness of the puffy clouds toward the mountains they were approaching; yet the transport was not slowing down nor increasing in altitude to fly over the peaks. She bit her lip before calling out to Captain Gabe in a panicked voice. When he didn't respond, Sherpa shrieked, "Stop! We're gonna crash!" Just when collision seemed certain, the mountain wall peeled open, the transport landed inside, and the mountain wall closed behind them—all in less than six seconds.

Lillian laughed at Sherpa's shocked reaction. "Some days it's really fun to be ruler," she remarked nonchalantly while stepping out of the transport.

Sherpa followed her mother, griping, "Couldn't ya have warned me about that? Sixteen is a bit young to have a heart attack! Darn it, I bit my lip so hard it's bleeding."

Ignoring the sarcasm, Lillian handed her a handkerchief. "Before we meet Dr. Lichtenstein, I need to handle an issue. On the ride here, I was speaking with the chancellor of the environment. The Agency has found conclusive proof that polar bears are not extinct, as we thought for the past 150 years, but we have to act quickly to save the last remaining families. Believe it or not, their fur is no longer white! When the polar caps shrank significantly, their coats adapted to a camouflage color of muddy browns. Will you be OK for a while?"

Sherpa blotted her bleeding lip and muttered, "This is just great—it's the day after my sixteenth birthday, and I have to spend it talking to some old, white-haired scientist."

Lillian remarked casually, "Oh, I don't think you'll mind talking to this particular scientist," and walked with her characteristic quick gait toward the Communications Room.

While Sherpa loved her mom, Lillian could drive her totally crazy! For starters, Lillian had lots of energy. Despite being younger and a good six inches taller, Sherpa sometimes had a hard time keeping up—not that she'd ever admit that to her shrimpy mother. Sherpa really hated it when people compared them. First of all they looked nothing alike, with the exception of their blue eyes. Her mom had short, blonde hair, and they had opposite taste in clothes—thank goodness for that.

Some days Sherpa couldn't decide whether there were more ups or downs associated with being the first kid. Over the past four years, she had met some really cool people, learned about a lot of different cultures by traveling the world, and lived in their awesome penthouse apartment. The biggest highlight, though, had to be lighting the torch for the 2308 Olympics hosted in Ethiopia. Sherpa had spent two weeks there and had a blast! The country was beautiful, there was constant entertainment, and the cities were rich with amazing architecture and lush landscape. Best of all, it was the first time medals were recorded under the new "Eastern World" and "Western World" designations. It came down to the wire, with literally the entire planet watching. Thanks to the final competition in a new sport called polling, the Western World topped the medal count by one.

Despite the awesome stuff, being the daughter of Lillian, Ruler of the Western World, could really stink. All kids make mistakes, but Sherpa's were magnified, documented, and preserved for the entire galaxy to see. There was this one time that she had wanted to go to a party, and her mother wouldn't let her go. Thinking she was really sly, she snuck out past the robots without getting caught and went to the party. The plan may have worked, but some paparazzi took her picture and instantly sent it to her mother's communicator—and to the communicators of practically everyone else in the Western World. Lillian was waiting by the door when Sherpa tiptoed in. Needless to say, Sherpa was grounded for a long time. And to make matters even worse, it was a terrible picture. Her eyes were half closed, and she had a huge pimple on her chin!

But the worst experience EVER happened when the boy Sherpa had a huge crush on finally asked her to a school dance. Simon was captain of the academy's flying football team and was soooooo cute. She was over-the-moon excited and spent hours picking out the ideal dress and practiced a dozen different hairstyles. She agonized over whether to wear her long, black, curly hair up or leave it down. She wanted the night to be perfect! Two days before the dance, she excitedly walked to meet Simon by the lunchroom.

Simon was leaning against the wall, hanging out with some flying football buddies, and he didn't see her approach the group. Sherpa overheard him taunting, "Tomorrow night you guys will be paying up! I won the bet to get my picture taken with the Ruler of the Western World. Too bad it means I have to take that brainiac Sherpa to the dance; I would rather have taken Katia—she's hot!"

The rest of the school day was a total blur. Her feelings smashed into at least a million pieces, Sherpa sobbed into her pillow wishing she had never been born. After running out of tears, she called Amy, who had some great advice on how to handle "The Simon Situation." By the time the girls finished the conversation, Sherpa actually looked forward to the next day at school.

She waited until Simon was once again surrounded by his buddies and made her approach. "Simon, it was very sweet of you to ask me to the dance, but I've had a better offer. See ya." With that she turned and walked away listening, with extreme pleasure, to Simon's friends laugh at him. The next day at the dance, Sherpa had a great time with Amy's cousin, who happened to go to another school. "Amy was totally right. Living well is the best revenge!"

A loud noise interrupted her walk down memory lane. She looked around quickly and realized that the Technology Lab was unlike any building she'd ever seen before. Sherpa's head spun as she took in the amazing sights and sounds of the lab. "Nothing in the old twentieth-century sci fi movies could come close to this!" she thought with astonishment. The lab was a hub of activity with scientists, robots—and HuBots!

Sherpa walked toward a group of scientists who were conducting tests on various HuBot prototypes. Sherpa had heard that scientists were working on technology to make robots more lifelike, but she had no idea it had really happened. She had to look closely to tell the difference between the human scientists and mechanical HuBots.

One of the scientists approached Sherpa and introduced herself. "Hi, I'm Dr. Cate. You must be Sherpa. Pretty cool, huh! Obviously robots are still used for simple tasks, but we needed them to do more. So over the past several years, we have focused our resources on developing the first generation of HuBots that actually make decisions and have reasoning ability. Would you like to be part of this experiment?"

Sherpa hesitated. "Sure…as long as it won't hurt."

Dr. Cate giggled. "No, it won't hurt. We are currently testing the ability of HuBots to interact normally with humans. This test is actually a joint experiment with the Intelligence Agency in a project to eventually replace human spies with HuBots."

Walking Sherpa toward a group of HuBots, Dr. Cate announced proudly, "We just achieved a huge breakthrough. HuBots look human, but they lack true emotion. Since astute people will eventually figure that out, we had to enhance the ability of HuBots to quickly gain information, and then get out fast. This generation of HuBots gets all their information electronically by downloading whatever is around. They can be in the vicinity of a communicator and immediately get access to everything in it. Or they can walk into a building, and all the information from electronic devices will automatically be sent to the databases at the Intelligence Agency for analysis."

"Wow, that's high-tech osmosis. Guess I better be careful what I say in my diary," Sherpa said apprehensively.

"Don't worry, this technology is only to be used to ensure Western World security. But yes, assuming you use a Diary app in your communicator, they could access the data." Pointing to an attractive, brown-haired prototype wearing large sunglasses, Dr. Cate said, "We named her Jackie, and her mission is to work undercover getting information out of the bad guys without their even realizing it. Jackie, this is Sherpa."

The HuBot Jackie sauntered over to Sherpa and extended her hand. "Hello, darling. You are quite cute, but you simply must work on your ability to match clothes better! That shirt is way too wrinkled, and those shoes went out of style 1.28 years ago."

Sherpa was irritated now; it was the second slam on her clothes today. Her mother had actually made a similar comment about her shirt while entering the transport. She shot Dr. Cate a look that screamed, "You have GOT to be kidding me!"

Dr. Cate quickly said, "Sorry, Sherpa. We are in the process of loading Jackie with all types of data on current clothing styles since she will be undercover as a high-powered executive in the fashion industry. Our next challenge is how to program the concept of tact into the HuBots."

Sherpa unloaded her frustration. "Look, maybe my shirt is a little crumpled, but it's like mac-n-cheese: total comfort, and I love it! Perhaps in addition to loading Jackie with fashion data for adults, you should also load her with data regarding what kids like to wear."

Dr. Cate immediately walked back to the testing area and started talking excitedly with another scientist. "Why didn't we think of that?" Quickly immersed back in her work, she totally forgot about Sherpa.

Sherpa shook her head and walked back to join her mother. "Scientists…"

The door to the Communications Room slid open, and Lillian exited with a huge smile on her face. "The Environmental Agency was actually able to develop a vast shield around the polar bears and lower the temperature to create more snow. The bears will never know humans are around. Hopefully this environment will allow them to survive and continue to breed. The technology is incredible." She sighed happily. "OK, time to focus now on the reason why we are here."

Lillian approached a guy who looked more like a surfer than a scientist. He was tall and gorgeous, and Sherpa was pretty sure she could make out some nice-sized muscles under his white lab coat.

"Dr. Lichtenstein, I'd like to introduce my daughter, Sherpa."

Dr. Lichtenstein brushed his blonde hair out of his eyes, crossed his arms in front of his chest in the standard Western World greeting, and bowed. "Welcome to the Technology Laboratory. You are going to love the RTD and how it enables time travel."

Chapter

2

The RTD

"YOU ARE DR. LICHTENSTEIN? WHERE IS the white hair? RTD? Time travel?" The words tumbled uncontrolled out of Sherpa's mouth like marbles spilled from a bag.

Lillian chuckled at Sherpa's surprise. "Sweetheart, this is all tied to your potential future appointment as chancellor of positivity. Dr. Lichtenstein has developed an enhanced time travel device. While I commissioned the Technology Laboratory to conduct this work about nine months ago and have been given regular updates, this is the first time I've actually seen the finished product."

Dr. Lichtenstein said, "Madame Ruler, I am so excited to finally show you and Sherpa the outcome of all our hard work. I'll explain more in depth while we walk to my office—I know you won't be disappointed. Here is the RTD!" He pulled a circular device out of his pocket that was about the circumference of a tangerine but only a half inch deep. He handed it to Lillian.

Lillian held the platinum material in her hand and turned it over several times. Nothing happened.

Sherpa could tell her mother was not happy. Lillian had that tightness to her jaw that occurred right before she let loose on someone. "You spent nine months developing a chunk of metal?"

Dr. Lichtenstein pumped his arm in the air. "Yes! It worked!"

"Excuse me? Dr. Lichtenstein, I think you need to explain what is going on," Lillian commanded.

"Madame Ruler, during the development process, we realized that if the RTD ever got into the wrong hands, it would be disastrous for the fate of the world. So we programmed the only two RTDs in existence to work with just two people. Obviously, I need to use it from a development perspective."

Sherpa asked, "Who is the other person who can use it?"

Lillian turned to Sherpa. "You."

"Huh?" was the only response that Sherpa could think of.

Lillian handed the RTD to Sherpa. "I have chosen you to time travel back to the early twenty-first century and use this top secret RTD."

Sherpa held the circular device in her palm. Like a perfectly sized glove, it was designed to fit in her hand exclusively. As she wrapped her fingers around the disc, the platinum on the front side disappeared, and the RTD was alive with color. Sherpa had never seen anything like this in her entire life. She looked quizzically at her mom.

"I'll explain the background later. We need to use the time today with Dr. Lichtenstein to understand the features of the RTD." Lillian directed her attention back to the scientist. "Please continue."

"Gladly! My team has worked around the clock for the past nine months developing this device. I had people work on various elements; however, for security purposes, I am the only person who knows all its capabilities."

"What does RTD stand for?"

"Sorry, Sherpa, sometimes I get ahead of myself. An RTD is a Reality Tracking Device. It provides direct access to understand exactly what really is going on with another person—what makes up his or her reality." He took the RTD out of Sherpa's hand and pointed to the lights. "It's quite simple. The display screen shows issues that person is dealing with now. The cool thing is the RTD can also rewind scenes in the person's life if you need to understand what happened in the past. It's like watching a movie of someone's life. This will enable you figure out what's really going on and how you may be able to help."

Dr. Lichtenstein stopped and pulled another thing-amajig out of his white lab coat pocket; it was a small rectangular card. He tossed the card up, and it expanded into a large display screen and hung in the air a few feet from where they were standing. "Pretty cool, huh? I came up with the prototype for the Instascreen when I was studying to become a scientist. I was only twelve years old, so my intent was to use it to play games or watch sports whenever and wherever I wanted. Anyway, since the RTD display is too small for us to huddle around, I'll project the images on this large screen."

"What will you show us?" asked Sherpa.

"This is a real-life example to explain how the RTD works. I'm really ticked off with my friend Andy; he's also a scientist here. He's blown me off the past few times we've made plans to get together. Then he'll pick a fight for no reason and act as if it's my fault. Before I started this research, I would have assumed he was just being an idiot and ignored him. However, developing the RTD has taught me that people's perceptions of their reality can make them act differently from normal."

He spoke the name "Andy Chou" into the RTD, and the trio turned their attention to the floating screen. Andy was sitting in a chair next to a hospital bed, holding the hand of an elderly man. With a single tear running down his cheek, Andy said, "Grandpa, the doctor doesn't think the treatment is working."

Sherpa looked up at Dr. Lichtenstein. He swallowed hard before explaining, "Andy and I have been friends since we were little. He always stood up for me when the other kids made fun of the 'boy genius.' He's really close to his grandpa. I knew Andy's grandpa was older and not in great health, but didn't know it was this bad. Guess that explains why Andy's blown me off and gets angry for no apparent reason."

Lillian gently said, "So I can imagine you are no longer angry with Andy since you understand 'the story behind the story'—his reality—and can choose to approach the situation differently."

"Yeah," Dr. Lichtenstein replied ruefully. "I need to let him know I'm really sorry about his grandpa. I'm actually relieved he's not mad at me." When he finished talking, he snapped his fingers, and the Instascreen shrank back down to the size of a business card and flew into his hand.

Sherpa wanted the Instascreen in a big way! "Could I keep that thing? It could come in handy sometime— like when I want to win the 'who has the best gizmo in the cosmos' contest."

"Sure." Dr. Lichtenstein handed it to her. "There are more in the supply cabinet, and actually it may be helpful when you time travel. But I'll get to that soon."

Sherpa's head was spinning as she tucked the Instascreen into her pocket.

As the three began walking, Dr. Lichtenstein continued his lecture. "In addition to simply observing scenes in a person's life, there are two other important features on the RTD. The first is that the RTD will display people's energy as glowing colors. As you know, colors have specific vibrations. We started with the ancient Indian art of chakras and aura reading and simplified the color process for use in the RTD. A person with a white glow is pretty happy. Someone with a dark-red glow is mad, sad or sick. A gray glow means someone either has done or is about to do something bad or unhealthy. However, watch out for black glows. They are reserved for really bad dudes."

"Wow, I'll be able to see a person's energy field. The color white really gives new meaning to 'having good vibes!' What is the other important feature?" giggled Sherpa, who noticed Lillian had stepped away to speak with a HuBot prototype.

He flashed a grin. "I was waiting for you to ask. This is so wickedly cool. You can use the RTD to move into someone else's experience! This is the time travel element of the RTD; we call them 'Hops.' The RTD will even modify your clothing to the appropriate time period or event. Early in the testing, we had to send transports to pick up our test scientists because the RTD return function wasn't working right, but we fixed the bugs, and now it operates perfectly."

Sherpa was skeptical. "How does time travel work?"

Before he could respond, Lillian walked back toward the pair and interrupted. "Sherpa, I have to head back to the capital to deal with an emergency tied to this project. Tonight over dinner, I'll explain your assignment and how it could ultimately lead to your appointment as chancellor of positivity." She turned toward the scientist, crossed her arms, and bowed. "On behalf of the Western World, I thank you. Also convey my sincere gratitude to your team. You all have made a huge contribution toward the future of our world. Dr. Lichtenstein, continue educating my daughter about the features of the RTD. Time is of the essence."

He crossed his arms and bowed. "Thank you, Madame Ruler. I will."

Sherpa was so excited her mom left. The thought of being left alone with Dr. Lichtenstein caused a butterfly explosion in her stomach. She was still trying to figure out how old he was. Maybe eighteen? Plus, he was actually taller than she! Bonus!

Sherpa and Dr. L continued walking toward his office. When they arrived, he motioned her in. Sherpa observed that it looked more like a bedroom than the office of a genius scientist, well just minus the bed. The walls were constantly changing with various sports scenes including soccer, polling, surfing, and flying football. A snowboard leaned against the back corner, and there were two reclining chairs in the middle of the room.

"Where is your desk?" asked Sherpa.

"Don't need one. The walls are my computer screen and data storage. I'll show you my latest project—I'm working on an algorithm to develop the concept of tact in the HuBots."

"You need to work hard on that project," said Sherpa, still stinging a bit from her interaction with the HuBot Jackie.

"I heard about Jackie. Sorry about that." He then commanded, "Activate program—HuBots Playing Nice!"

A female voice asked, "Password, please."

As Dr. Lichtenstein responded with the password "Boarding," the walls immediately switched from sporting scenes to a bunch of numbers, letters, and figures. Sherpa had no clue as to their meaning. It could have been written in Atlantian for all she knew.

"You realize that based on seeing your snowboard in the corner, your password is pretty easy to guess?"

Dr. Lichtenstein said, "It actually doesn't matter what word I say. I could have said, 'lima beans,' and had the same reaction. The system reads my voice and conducts a body mass check and a retinal scan. The only time I've ever had problems was after participating in an extreme boarding competition between the Eastern and Western Worlds. In one weekend, I lost my voice and six pounds. If not for the retinal scan, I would have had to use the backup password system. Man, those Eastern World dudes were good. They smoked me."

"I don't get it—brilliant scientist and extreme snowboarder? Don't those activities seem to contradict each other?"

He shrugged. "Nah. When I get stuck on a problem, I need to get my mind off of the issue for a short time. Usually while in the middle of a jump, the answer pops into my head."

"I would have taken you more for a surfer."

"Actually, surfing is my passion. I modified my surfboard to double as a snowboard since the board is programmed to anticipate my next motions. Keeps me vertical longer."

Sherpa pictured Dr. L with no shirt and running on a white sand beach with his board. No wonder his hair looked highlighted, with all that time in the sun! She came back to reality when he turned toward her, his eyes twinkling with excitement, and said, "You asked earlier how the RTD works. Sometimes experience is better than explanation. Let's take a test drive with the

RTD." He grabbed her hand and pressed the blue button on the RTD.

The next thing Sherpa knew, she was transported back in time nine hundred years to the 1600s. She was wearing a long, poufy, lace dress and sitting next to Dr. Lichtenstein, who was also in clothing appropriate to the timeframe. They were riding in a carriage pulled by two chestnut-brown Morgan horses. "Nice wig," she teased.

He replied a little awkwardly, "I told you the RTD was programmed to provide the right dress for the period or occasion. You should have seen me in a test case back to Roman times."

While Dr. L reviewed the RTD display, Sherpa enjoyed a very pleasant daydream involving him wearing a toga. The carriage abruptly stopped.

"Mr. Newton!" Dr. Lichtenstein called out as he handed the reins to Sherpa and jumped out of the carriage. Isaac Newton stopped and turned to the carriage. "Sir, I have a message for you from Mr. Edmond Halley. He requests the honor of your presence in the apple orchard in order to tell you about a magnificent comet he saw in the night sky."

Isaac Newton said, "Thank you, young man. I will indeed go meet my friend Mr. Halley...though an apple orchard is a strange place to meet." As Mr. Newton walked away, Dr. Lichtenstein returned to the carriage, held Sherpa's hand, and pressed the red button on the RTD. Instantly Sherpa found herself back at the laboratory wearing her still-wrinkled twenty-fourth-century clothing.

Dr. Lichtenstein was ecstatic. "I just spoke with the most famous scientist who ever lived!" Seeing yet another confused look on Sherpa's face, he patiently explained, "Isaac Newton had a revelation about gravity while in an apple orchard. On the day we went back in time, the RTD told me he made a decision not to walk near the apple orchard. Our interaction got him there. When Edmond Halley obviously didn't show up, he had time to think, the apple fell on his head, and voila, the concept of gravity was born!"

"How come we weren't credited in any stories about the famous apple falling on his head?"

"A failsafe was built into the RTD system—people you interact with will never remember you after the fact. However, they will remember the lesson you taught and general comments you made."

She grinned. "Too bad. It would have been fun to read about the guy in the funky wig who saved gravity. Seriously though, how did the RTD even know that Isaac Newton didn't plan to go to the apple orchard in the first place?"

"Fantastic query! I love it when people question things. This one I can't really explain; you need to see it for yourself."

Dr. Lichtenstein motioned for Sherpa to sit down in one of the recliners. He then sat down in the other. "I promise to give the short answers and spare you all the technical jargon." He then commanded, "Activate RTD Notification Program."

The walls once again changed. Only this time there were no undecipherable formulas circling the room. Instead the walls were filled with waves of blue light. As her eyes adjusted, Sherpa could tell that the waves were comprised of many shades of blue, ranging from navy to royal to the color of the crystal-clear water in the Caribbean Ocean. Periodically a point of red light would appear in the midst of blues.

Dr. Lichtenstein was silent while Sherpa took it all in. Finally she spoke. "It's absolutely beautiful—mesmerizing in fact—but what is it?"

"What you are seeing is universal energy. In school, kids learn about various types of energy such as kinetic, light, thermal, and electromagnetic. My team has developed a way to see energy. I'll be the first to admit that we don't yet understand even a fraction of what we are observing. To make a long story short, during the beta studies with the RTD, I noticed the correlation between situations where people needed help and the red points of light. So we downloaded all recorded history into the program and wrote an algorithm to send an alert to the RTD when an interaction must occur to prevent history from changing in a negative way."

"I'm not normally at a loss for words, but this has blown me away," said Sherpa incredulously.

"Your main mission is to help kids learn to be positive and make good decisions. Madame Ruler will explain more about that to you tonight. But a side job is to ensure history stays on course."

"Awesome! While I wasn't crazy about physics class, I am an absolute history junkie. I have always wanted to meet Cleopatra and Gandhi and…"

Dr. Lichtenstein interrupted. "Wait a minute, Sherpa. It's not a toy. The RTD is not intended to change world history for personal gain or even just because you are curious and want to meet someone. You can't mess around with history. It was fantastic that I got to meet Isaac Newton, but I would never have chosen that.

Plus, you can't do anything to draw attention to yourself by the bad guys. Look, I have to go now, and you've already had a lot to absorb today. I'll see you tomorrow, and we'll continue your training. OK?" He put out his hand.

Sherpa disappointedly dropped the RTD into his palm. "OK."

Dr. Lichtenstein ordered a robot that had silently rolled up to his office door, "Take Sherpa to the transport. She is returning to the capital."

During the short flight back to the apartment, Sherpa felt exhausted, invigorated, confused, and excited, all at the same time. She had always wanted adventure—now she may have more than she could ever imagine. She also couldn't stop thinking about Dr. Lichtenstein.

Chapter

The Assignment

OVER DINNER, SHERPA ENTHUSIASTICALLY described the details of her experiences at the lab and her observations of Dr. Lichtenstein. "Mom, this guy is brilliant! I'm used to being the smartest kid in class, but there is no way I can compete with him. I still can't believe I met Sir Isaac Newton!"

"Sweetheart, I know you are excited, but I need for you to listen very carefully to what I am about to tell you. Outside of Dr. Lichtenstein and my intelligence chancellor, no one else in the Western World is aware of what I'm about to share with you."

Considering the grave look on Lillian's face, Sherpa wasn't so sure she really wanted to hear what was coming next.

"As you know, when the treaty was signed in 2306 to signify the End of all Wars, world political leaders decided that in order to prevent smaller countries from violating the terms of the treaty, it was necessary to consolidate world leadership into two large regions—the Eastern World and the Western World. The vast majority of world leaders were quite content with the fact that Earth would never experience the disastrous consequences of war. However, a few very unhappy dictators could not face losing their power because of world peace. Last year our Intelligence Agency learned these dictators, led by General Aveel, used their resources to invent a time-travelling device. We think they plan to go back in time and breed negativity among kids. Their hypothesis is that if kids learn to become negative and make poor decisions, this behavior will continue as adults. Negativity will breed negativity across generations; over the course of three hundred years, the world will not desire world peace, and the 2306 treaty of the End of all Wars will never be signed. If this happens, humankind as we know it will cease to exist."

As the magnitude of what her mother was telling her sank in, Sherpa felt a knot in the pit of her stomach and bit her lip hard. Used to the secrecy that came with her mother's job, she confusedly asked, "Why are you telling me all this? You must have your entire Intelligence Agency working on stopping General Aveel and his cronies."

"Actually, no. I'm convinced he has spies planted everywhere. If word leaked out of our knowledge about General Aveel's plot, we may not be able to stop him. As I said earlier, only four people know: me, the intelligence chancellor, Dr. Lichtenstein, and now… you."

Sherpa really hoped that her mother was exaggerating, but when she saw the look on Lillian's face, she knew this was real, and very, very serious.

"While our Intelligence Agency has some excellent spies, they are not prepared to go back in time to help kids. You are the right person."

Sherpa jumped up from her chair and walked away from the table. "Whoa, Mom! This is a way bigger responsibility than I can handle! In school, the worst thing to happen was to flunk an assignment. It sure sounds as if the consequences are huge if I flunk this! There has got to be someone better equipped than I am for saving the world. Couldn't Dr. Liechtenstein mix some superhero DNA with some Mother Teresa DNA and create a HuBot to handle this?"

Lillian chuckled. "Sherpa, believe it or not, I actually considered something like that. But HuBots can't feel any emotion. They are wired to make analytical decisions based solely on data. We all know emotions are huge factors in decision making. HuBots can't touch people's hearts and minds—but you can. You've also made your share of mistakes over time and can understand where kids are coming from."

"I'm not sure whether to feel praised or insulted," Sherpa said, annoyed with the comment. Sometimes her mother could totally drive her nuts.

"Sherpa," Lillian said gently as she touched her daughter's cheek, "You told me this morning that you have prepared to be the chancellor of positivity. I have complete trust in your motives and faith in your abilities. Your drive and energy is a necessity for the adventure that will change your life—and potentially the lives of everyone on the planet. The reason I had to leave the Technology Lab early today was because the intelligence chancellor learned that General Aveel has accelerated his plan. We originally thought there would be time for at least three weeks of training for you. That is now cut short."

"Uh, how short?"

"You start tomorrow."

"What!" Sherpa exclaimed, her heart pounding so loudly she figured the people on the 199th floor could hear it and would start complaining about the noise.

"Don't worry. You will still have preparation, but it will be on-the-job training. You'll start using the RTD technology to work with kids throughout the past millennium. This will give you some practice and should help reinforce that despite societal, economic, cultural, and generational differences, all kids face the same type of issues." Lillian hesitated a moment. "Sherpa, I know you two don't have any secrets, but in this case, for her safety and yours, you cannot tell Amy."

Sherpa suddenly felt very overwhelmed. How could she not tell her BFF! Resigned to this fate, she asked quietly, "Then what do I do?"

"Ultimately, you need to land in the early twenty-first century; we believe that is where General Aveel plans to start breeding negativity. There you will find who you are looking for—the two kids who will start the chain of events that ultimately will save our world."

Chapter

The Practice Run

AFTER A SLEEPLESS NIGHT, SHERPA FOUND herself back on the transport in flight to the hidden Technology Laboratory. She still didn't like the sensation of almost crashing into a mountain. And she really didn't like being told that returning to the year 2310 was not an option until she completed her mission in the early twenty-first century. The intelligence chancellor had determined it was too risky for her to bounce back and forth from the past, but Sherpa had other priorities as well. "Spies are everywhere—whatever! He's not the one who is missing out on spring break at the beach.

Amy and I even bought the cutest bathing suits!" She hoped her friend wouldn't be too mad after watching the video message giving a lame excuse for ditching their vacation.

As she exited the transport carrying her favorite ginormous purple-and-gold purse, Dr. Lichtenstein was waiting. "For someone about to embark on saving the human race, you don't look very wide awake. What are you carrying in that huge purple bag, anyway?"

"You are seriously asking me that question? I just found out yesterday that I'm traveling through time with no ETA on my return. I will need a few things for the journey," she said, her sarcastic tone broken up by a yawn.

He laughed and handed Sherpa a mug of hot chocolate. "Your mom warned me you are not a morning person."

Sherpa blew into the cup and studied the good-looking scientist. She had spent much of her sleepless night researching him. His mom ran a large company, and his dad, a former professional flying football player, kept their life running smoothly despite the chaos associated with eight active kids. Dr. Troy Lichtenstein, the youngest of the eight, had graduated with his PhD at age fifteen and was recruited right out of college to work at the secret Technology Lab. Now, three years later, he had at least a hundred patents and inventions under his belt. She wondered, "How can a guy have an off-the-chart IQ, be good at sports, AND look so darn cute? Maybe after this saving the world stuff is done, I can find out if he has a girlfriend!"

Dr. Liechtenstein handed her the RTD. She looked down at the small circular device in her hand—still amazed by the technology and the power the technology enabled.

"Any enhancements we make to my RTD here at the lab will automatically come to your RTD. We are always developing new apps; some big improvements and some just for fun. For example, when version four is launched, you'll be able to use your RTD on HuBots," he explained.

"Wait a minute. I'm supposed to be going back in time, not to the future. HuBots don't exist in the past. You are just developing them now."

"The intelligence chancellor believes that General Aveel is creating his own version of HuBots to travel back to the past. Guess no one told you that?"

"Uh, that would be a big fat no! How am I supposed to be successful? Me against a small army is not good odds. And isn't there more instruction? It's like jumping into a pool without knowing how to swim. It doesn't seem quite right that I had more training to be a capital tour guide than I've had to save the world!" Sherpa threw up her hands in frustration, spilling hot chocolate on the floor.

While a robot scurried over to clean up the mess, Dr. Lichtenstein explained, "As you start using the RTD, you'll find that it's an amazing secret weapon. Aveel's scientists are good—time travel is not an easy code to crack. But they don't have an RTD. Your advantage comes with the other things the RTD can do. You will essentially know everything you need about a situation. Also, remember HuBots don't have feelings and emotions."

Her face lit up. "That means a HuBot can't generate colors! That's how I'll know if someone is a regular human or a hunk of metal."

Dr. L slapped Sherpa a high five. "Exactly."

"What else do I need to know?" she asked.

"You think that we just met yesterday, but during the RTD development period, I studied you pretty closely."

Taking a step back toward the door, she asked warily, "What are you, some kind of a stalker?"

"Not in a creepy sense, but I suppose the term 'stalking' is somewhat accurate from a scientific standpoint. Remember when I told you that I modified my snow-surf board to anticipate my next movement?"

"Yes…"

"Well, I applied that same concept of anticipating your moves to develop the RTD specifically for your needs. I collected your school transcripts, old interviews you gave, and pretty much everything else I could find about you since the day you were born and ran the data through our programs."

"Oh, come on, that's ridiculous. You don't know me, and you have no idea how I'll react to situations."

"Is that so?" Dr. Lichtenstein tried to stifle a laugh. "You bite your bottom lip every time you get really nervous. You are smart but like to test the limits and are OK with breaking a few rules. Your middle school years were not always fun; some days you came home crying. You love to be the center of attention sometimes but not all the time. And right now you want nothing more than to blow me off, fly in the transport to the beach, and run barefoot until your legs turn to jelly. Then you'd go eat a huge plate of french fries and drink root beer while complaining to your best friend, Amy, about the crazy scientist who thinks he can anticipate your next move."

Sherpa stared in disbelief, but she wasn't entirely ready to admit defeat. "You neglected to mention that I dip my fries in barbeque sauce instead of ketchup." She also wanted to change the subject. "Not to sound egotistical, but I am the daughter of Lillian, Ruler of the Western World. I do travel quite a bit with my mother. At some point, people will notice I'm gone."

"I don't know all the details, that's the job of the Intelligence Agency. I think that the official line will be that you are ready for a break from the limelight and are going to an undisclosed location to start medical school courses."

"Geez, couldn't they have come up with a more exciting story? Like I wanted to go to an Ashram in old India and become a yogi? Or I needed to discover myself while backpacking through the Eastern World? The Intelligence Agency really needs to work on creativity."

He shrugged his shoulders and handed her the RTD. "You're right, though; it would be helpful for you to have a bit more training. How about we do another practice hop together like the one we did with Sir Isaac Newton? This time, how about you take the lead? Press the blue button, and the RTD Notification Program will take us where we are needed."

Not wanting him to know how relieved she felt, Sherpa simply nodded and said, "Good idea." She took hold of his hand and pressed the blue flashing button, and instantly she and Dr. L were standing on the side-walk of a small town. She was in a checkered dress, and he was wearing an old-fashioned business suit and a hat. Her ginormous purple purse had been replaced with a small, black pocketbook.

"Where are we?" she asked.

Dr. Lichtenstein pointed to the RTD. "Here is a summary of where we are and why it's necessary to be here. It's not safe to use the Instascreen in public, so we'll need to both look at the display on the RTD."

This was the closest she had ever stood to him—he smelled so good! Trying to ignore the butterflies that now left her stomach to invade her entire body, she said, "We are in a small town in Ohio in the early 1940s. Ohmigosh, we need to help Neil Armstrong when he was a kid! He was the first man to walk on the moon!"

"What else does it say? Why are we here?" he asked.

"According to the RTD, Mr. Armstrong is about to make a serious mistake that will impact his ability to get into his college. If he doesn't get into that particular college, he'll never end up with NASA and won't walk on the moon. Even more important, if he's not there, he'll never be able to make certain decisions that would actually save the lives of everyone on Apollo Eleven." The history buff in Sherpa added, "Back in the 1960s, the race to the moon was so significant that thousands of kids became interested in science. If man doesn't make it to the moon in the 1960s, the destiny of lots of people could be negatively impacted."

"So Sherpa, what is your next step?"

She took a deep breath and exhaled slowly. "According to the RTD, the young Neil Armstrong is being bullied by some older kids. The poor kid has a lot of the color gray around him—he's definitely in trouble.

He believes if he does what the bullies want, they'll leave him and his sister alone. What he doesn't know is that he will be caught, kicked out of Boy Scouts, and will never become an Eagle Scout. His future will continue to unravel. He is now at the drugstore. The bullies ordered him to steal cigarettes."

She crinkled her nose in disgust. "I'm so glad those nasty things don't exist anymore. I mean don't exist back in 2310...I've gotta work on my terminology with the time travel thing."

As they walked toward the drugstore, Dr. Lichtenstein asked, "Have you thought about what you'll say?"

"No, but I'm pretty good at figuring out what to say when I need to. If I think too much in advance, I may overanalyze the situation."

Dr. Lichtenstein nodded approvingly. "It's good you know your style and how you best operate. Let's go!"

Sherpa pushed the blue button, and the next thing she knew, she was sitting on a stool at the soda fountain in the back of the drugstore. Dr. L was nowhere to be seen. She glanced at the picture on the RTD before placing it in her black pocketbook. "Darn, this purse is small," she thought. The boy sitting on the stool next to her looked just like the picture. It was Neil. He was nervously tapping his fingers on the counter. She took a deep breath and plunged into the deep end.

"Hi, I'm Sherpa. What's your name?"

"Uh. I'm Neil," replied the boy.

"Can I buy you an ice cream sundae, Neil?"

His eyes widened. "Thank you, ma'am. That would be swell!"

The soda fountain clerk, clad in white and wearing a white, pointy hat, scooped ice cream into two bowls, loaded them up and slid them across the counter. Sherpa took a bite, licked her lips, then asked, "You look as if you have a lot on your mind right now; want to talk about it?"

"NO!" he replied, before softening his response a bit with, "I'm fine."

"Yikes." thought Sherpa. "What am I supposed to do now? Dr. L didn't tell me it would be this hard…" She shifted on her stool and tried again. "Neil, I've learned that nobody always has all the answers and everyone needs a little help now and then. Sometimes just talking about problems helps."

He was silent for a moment as he stuck the spoon into the whipped cream and played with the cherry. "Some kids want me to do something, and if I don't, they'll keep hounding my sister and me. I know it's not right, but…" his voice trailed off.

Sherpa finished his sentence: "But doing what they want would make your life easier right now."

He nodded.

After taking another bite of her ice cream, Sherpa said, "You don't need to tell me, but ask yourself one question: Could what you are thinking about doing hurt you or others? In other words, could you get in trouble, and is it worth it?"

Neil finished his ice cream and let out a big sigh as he jumped off the stool. "Yes. If I got caught, I would be in a huge amount of trouble. My dad would kill me. I think I need to figure out another way. Thank you for the sundae, ma'am."

Sherpa opened her pocketbook, paid for the sundaes, and took a quick peek at the RTD. The gray color was gone; Neil was now surrounded by white. She grinned. "You are very welcome." As she stood up to leave, she felt compelled to add, "Hey, did you know that there will be a full moon tonight? Can you imagine how swell it would be to actually walk on the moon?"

After ducking behind an aisle of cough syrup, she pressed the red button and ended up back in Dr. Lichtenstein's office at the Technology Lab. He was kicked back in one of the two recliner chairs, watching a replay of the recent polling world championships. She climbed into the other recliner and sat down cross-legged.

"Where did you go?" she asked.

"The RTD knew I wasn't needed, so it sent me back to the lab. By the way, did you like the ice cream?"

"It was yummalicious! Wait, how did you know I ate ice cream?" she asked suspiciously.

"I could make up an elaborate story about having a monitoring device on you, but the simple answer is that you have a little bit of chocolate on the corner of your mouth," he said as he reached over to wipe it off. "So how did it feel?"

Trying to ignore the wave of excitement that overcame her when he touched her cheek, Sherpa answered, "Honestly, it felt good. And you are right; the RTD was pretty easy to use. Fortunately Neil didn't ask me what he should do. I'm not sure what I would have told him."

"In all our testing of the RTD, we found that most people already know deep down what they should or should not do. Sometimes they just need a little help to figure it out," Dr. Lichtenstein said.

Sherpa thought about his statement for a moment. "Hmmm, that actually makes a lot of sense. And it makes me feel so much better. I had no idea how I could come up with solutions for all these people I'm supposed to help."

Dr. Lichtenstein turned toward her, and Sherpa could swear his blue eyes seemed to look right through her. "Remember, Sherpa, you are a guide, not an instructor."

"Honestly, I don't know the difference between a guide and an instructor. I always thought they were the same thing."

"No—they are very different. Let me toss up the Instascreen, and we can look up the definitions," said Dr. L as he reached in his lab coat pocket.

"Wait a minute," said Sherpa. "I could look up Webster's definition myself if I thought that would help. Tell me what YOU think the differences are between instructors and guides."

Dr. Lichtenstein sank back in his chair. "OK, well, I think that a guide supports people and provides assistance as necessary. An instructor provides step-by-step directions how to do something a certain way. Let me think of an analogy...I know. In school, there were certain subjects like math that required formulas and equations to be specifically explained and done in a sequence. So my teachers were instructing me what to do and how to follow their directions."

"I get it—instructors tend to dictate precisely what needs to be done for a certain reason."

"Exactly. Several years ago when I wanted to learn to snowboard in heavy powder, I went up the mountain with some experienced guys. They showed me some basics and watch-outs, but I had to learn my own style. I fell a bunch at the beginning but eventually got my groove—although you had better believe that I followed a few of their instructions, such as staying away from the side of the cliff and watching out for trees!"

"All right, that makes sense. The boarding dudes were guiding you. What makes me really nervous is when people want step-by-step instructions and I don't have the answers!" Sherpa said.

"Trust me, your mom is a smart lady. If Madame Ruler didn't think you were ready, you wouldn't be going. This will be an amazing experience for you. You will meet people who will teach you as much as you teach them."

"But what if I get into a situation I can't handle?" Sherpa asked in alarm.

"Don't worry. I built in an additional feature that no one else knows, not even my team." He held up the RTD. "If you get into really big trouble, insert a tiny pin into this hole on the side. The RTD will become in essence a time-travel phone. Unfortunately, you can't take your communicator, but no matter what century you are in, you'll be able to reach me."

"The Intelligence Agency told me I cannot return to 2310 until the mission is completed. Yet the RTD returned us to the lab after each test hop. What is different?" Sherpa asked, hoping he could bend that rule for her. She really didn't want to miss spring break.

"The difference in the programming is that instead of returning to 2310, your RTD will continue to send you on these hops back in time. Remember the red points of light you saw in my office when we discussed the RTD notification process? The RTD has recognized events in the past where famous historical figures need help—but most of the time these famous folks will be kids. You'll practice your skills helping kids throughout the past millennium and ultimately end up where you need to be in the early twenty-first century."

"Right. I need to find the two kids who will ensure that the End of all Wars still happens. How will I know who they are and not mistake them for another practice hop?"

"You'll know." In typical surfer fashion, Dr. Troy Lichtenstein added, "Just ride the wave, Sherpa, and you'll be fine. Just ride the wave…"

Chapter

5

On Her Own

SHERPA FELT THE COOL METAL OF THE
RTD pressed next to her palm. Suddenly she felt very
alone and very tired. With false bravado, she tucked
the ginormous purple-and-gold purse under her arm,
waved to Dr. L, and pressed the blue button.

In the blink of an eye, she found herself on a deserted
beach. In her hands was a large basket. "Well," she
thought wryly, "guess I got spring break after all. I always
say, when in Rome do as the Romans do, and when on a
beach, dig your toes in the sand!" Sherpa spotted a row
of palm trees about three hundred yards away, which

created the perfect shade canapé. "I need a nap." She unrolled a large blanket she found in the basket and laid it on top of the warm, white sand. Sherpa plopped down, breathed in the salty sea air, and promptly fell asleep.

She was awakened by bright light in her eyes; she had slept so long that the sun shifted and her blanket was no longer in the shade. Still groggy, it took Sherpa a few moments to remember where she was and why she was there. But when the realization hit, it hit big. Speaking aloud to the empty beach, she mused, "Just three days ago, I was celebrating my sixteenth birthday. Now I'm supposed to help save the world. Holy cow…."

Opening the basket, she was thrilled to find it well stocked with food. Sherpa pulled out some red apples, a hunk of cheese, and flaky croissants. After taking a drink of cool water from a glass jar, she bit into a croissant. There were bits of chocolate inside the flaky pastry. "OK, I'll be able to manage this—whatever this is. And wherever I am now, at least I know the food is good."

While nibbling on the cheese, Sherpa looked around. The crystal-clear, blue water reminded her of the blue waves of energy in the RTD Notification Program. And the waves reminded her of surfing. And surfing reminded Sherpa of Dr. Lichtenstein. "All right, I admit I have a bit of a crush on him…he is two years older…but two years really isn't that much…but he did develop the time travel phone functionality if I need to reach him…so maybe he does like me? UGH! I'm doing exactly what I said I don't like to do—overanalyze." She jumped off the blanket. "I need a long run."

Sherpa had started running at age twelve because it was required for gym class, but she was quickly hooked after realizing that running helped her clear her mind. However, another upside was she could eat more chocolate and french fries. Only then did she look down at her outfit. "Wow, I must have really been out of it not to notice this!" She was wearing a very old-fashioned, navy-blue bathing suit with sleeves down to her wrists, a skirt that went to her knees, and pants underneath the skirt that were drawn in at the ankle. Trying to find the positive in what she considered a major fashion faux pas, she thought, "Well, at least the color looks good on me." It was obvious she was not yet in the twenty-first century. Since there was no way she could take a proper run in that get-up, Sherpa decided instead to walk along the water's edge. She tucked the RTD into a pocket in the skirt. "Wonder if this thing is waterproof?"

After strolling along the shore for a while, she noticed in the distance someone fishing. As she got closer, she realized the fisherman was a guy who looked to be about her age, or maybe a year older. "Bonjour, monsieur. Je m'appele Sherpa." Sherpa said to the fisherman. "Ohmigosh, I'm speaking French! And I don't even know French!" she thought.

He looked surprised to see her. "Bonjour, Mademoiselle. Je m'appele Gustave. I am not used to seeing many people on this beach."

"It is nice to meet you, Gustave. I am just visiting for a short time." Wanting to change the topic away from her, she asked, "Do you fish here often?"

"Not much," he replied. "I am enrolled at the university but thinking of quitting." Just then a fish was caught on his line. While he was distracted netting his catch, Sherpa took a quick peek at the RTD. Gustave was not just any college kid fisherman, this was Gustave Eiffel! As in the Eiffel Tower in Paris! The replica Eiffel Tower had been rebuilt in the twenty-second century after his original, constructed in 1889, had finally succumbed to age and rust. Poor Gustave was surrounded by red.

She thought, "OK, here I go, my first solo run. I can get rid of his red color…I think."

"What are you studying at the university?" Sherpa asked Gustave.

"I am studying engineering," he said glumly as he rebaited his hook and tossed the line in the water.

"It doesn't sound as if you like it very much. Is that why you want to quit school?" Sherpa asked.

"I like engineering and designing things, but I am bored with school!" he replied vehemently.

"A smart person once told me that there is so much to do in this world that if I'm bored, it is my own fault."

At first he looked offended, but as the words sank in, Gustave shook his head as if dusting off cobwebs. "You are absolutely right. I feel I'm in a rut and using the fact that I'm bored as an excuse not to do anything… except fish." He added with a slight smile, "But I do like fishing!"

"Have you thought what else you could do, besides fishing, to get you out of your rut?"

He shrugged.

Sherpa was starting to sweat underneath her ridiculously heavy full body swimsuit—partly from the heat of the sun, but partly because she was running out of ideas how to help the young Mr. Eiffel. Taking a deep breath, she continued asking questions. "Well then, what do you like? What inspires you?"

He thought for a moment. "I do love designing and understanding how pieces fit together. But I feel unbalanced, as if something is missing. I envy my friends who are studying philosophy. While I work equations, they read books on topics that make their minds soar!"

Sherpa was incredibly grateful at that moment that she was a history junkie. "So what's stopping you from doing both engineering and philosophy? Take a look at Leonardo Da Vinci. His interest in art, music, and sculpture enhanced his abilities as an engineer and inventor."

Sand flew in the air as Gustave jumped to his feet while snagging another fish. "Mon Dieu! Sherpa, you are right! I don't need to limit my interests! Merci beaucoup!"

Figuring this was a good time to leave, she said, "Au revoir, Gustave." As she walked back in the direction of her blanket and basket, she felt compelled to turn around and add, "Think how exciting it would be to design a building—or other engineering marvel—that gets named after you!"

Sherpa felt like giving herself a high five. Without looking at the RTD, she knew the color around Gustave Eiffel was white again. She was so proud of herself that her feet barely touched the sand the entire walk back. She actually thought about jumping in the waves but was afraid the volume of material in her swimsuit would suck her under the water. Not being quite ready for the RTD to take her to the next assignment, Sherpa decided to enjoy the scenery awhile longer. She was grateful that the beach was deserted, hoping that meant that none of General Aveel's spies were hanging around. While she wasn't sure when surfboards were invented, she sure did wish she were sharing this blanket with Dr. Lichtenstein.

While digging through the basket for more of those amazing chocolate croissants, she noticed a spiral-bound paper notebook and pencil nestled at the bottom. This particular notebook was beautifully decorated with a colorful pattern. Sherpa wasn't much into girly girl stuff, but the notebook was pretty. The novelty was what really intrigued her, though. She had seen paper notebooks in museums and occasionally at antique stores, but to hold an actual notebook was really cool. When everything went electronic back in the twenty-third century, bans were implemented regarding cutting down trees for general paper usage.

She placed the notebook next to her on the blanket, her mind swirling as she munched on the last croissant. So far, she had been successful with two RTD interactions—Neil Armstrong and Gustave Eiffel. While happy with a 100 percent success rate, Sherpa was still pretty nervous. She mused, "Whenever I doubt myself, Mom always asks the question, 'What worked well for you before?' How the heck do I duplicate success when I haven't a clue what continent or century I'll end up landing in? I need a *How to Fix History and Save the World Cookbook*." A light bulb went off in her head. "That's it—a manual! If the brilliant Dr. Lichtenstein couldn't provide one for me, then I need to create a manual of what works and what doesn't work."

Sherpa grabbed the colorful notebook and opened it to the front page. Expecting to find it entirely blank, she was shocked to see an inscription handwritten beautifully with gold ink. It read:

Sweetheart,

Things are not always as they seem. Trust yourself, be willing to take calculated risks, and above all, please be careful.

I Love You,
Mom

This gift surprised her. She knew her mom loved her—all moms are supposed to love their kids. But her mom wasn't exactly the sentimental type, and she was quite practical with gifts. What exactly did "Things are not always as they seem" mean? Sherpa had the sense that this notebook would come to be very important to her on this adventure.

Sherpa picked up the pencil, tried writing her name, and frowned. While she had taken handwriting in elementary school, she hadn't practiced it in years. Most writing was now done verbally or by thinking, but some communities in the far reaches of the Western World still used a form of typing. It was so much easier to think or just talk into the communicator and have everything automatically captured. Artificial intelligence had gotten so good over the past fifty years that the communicator would question if she really meant to use a certain concept. That feature had saved her butt a ton of times in school when she was writing research papers—usually at the last minute. "If I just had my communicator, writing a manual would be so much easier!"

Chapter

The Manual

WITH THE BACKGROUND MUSIC OF WAVES crashing and seagulls squawking, Sherpa turned the page, picked up the sharp pencil, and starting writing. Her penmanship eventually became more legible.

Insight #1: Sometimes a straightforward issue just requires providing a minor level of instruction.

What to do:

1. Suggest a specific action.

   ✔ Sir Isaac Newton: "Please go to the apple orchard."

Insight #2: Most people already have the answers inside of them. Sometimes they just need a little help realizing they are really not stuck after all.

What to do:

1. Ask open-ended questions and keep building on those questions. Sometimes questions will "plant a seed" or create a natural path for people to open their minds. Sometimes people just need to talk through an issue.

   ✔ Gustave Eiffel: "What inspires you?"

   ❖ Examples of open-ended questions include:

      ✔ "What do you like / dislike about ____?"

      ✔ "How do you feel when ____ happens?"

      ✔ "What else could you do?"

❖ Ask the Big Question: "Could what you are thinking about doing or not doing hurt yourself or other people?"

✔ Neil Armstrong: "Could you get in trouble, and is it worth it?"

Insight #3: Providing an analogy or similarity helps people relate to a situation.

<u>What to do:</u>

1. Think of an example involving a similar situation

✔ Gustave Eiffel: "If Leonardo Da Vinci could do it, why can't you?"

Insight #4: What works with one person may not work with another.

<u>What to do:</u>

1. Get a feel for each individual and how he or she may best respond—every person and situation is different and will require different questions or methods.

✔ Gustave Eiffel—He needed open-ended questions and the comparison to Leonardo Da Vinci.

Chapter

Good Intention...Bad Outcome

SHERPA CLOSED HER NOTEBOOK AND SIGHED. This was a start. She wasn't entirely comfortable with the assignment to save the world, but so far so good. She had even started writing a manual! The sky was turning beautiful shades of red and orange as the sun was starting to set, so Sherpa figured it was probably a good time to leave the beach via the RTD.

As she nestled the platinum circle in the palm of her hand, the lights immediately started flashing. This was her first opportunity to really play with the RTD. She had only pressed one button thus far, and she wondered how the rest worked. "I'm sure it won't hurt for me to select my next stop instead of the RTD picking all the time for me." She recalled that when Dr. Lichtenstein spoke the name of his friend Andy into the RTD, he pressed the red button instead of the blue.

In 2310, the terms equality and poverty were only discussed in history classes. Back in Sherpa's great-grandmother's generation, civilization finally figured out that prosperity was possible for all people. As a result, people were just people and had the ability to live as simply or luxuriously as they wished. This fundamental change in belief structure was instrumental in the success of negotiations leading up to the End of all Wars. War was simply no longer necessary.

Even though Sherpa's world was thankfully free of many types of hardship, she tried to appreciate that it had not always been that way. While pressing the red button, Sherpa spoke the name of a woman she admired tremendously who had lived through the Civil War era in America: "Harriet Tubman."

The next thing she knew, she was wearing a soiled cotton gown and kneeling in a cramped room with a bunch of other people similarly dressed. Small children were quietly whimpering, and the adults were listening intently to the instructions whispered by a woman with a commanding presence. "This has got to be Harriet Tubman," thought a shocked Sherpa, "and I must be in an Underground Railroad station!" It was pitch black outside when the group was herded out a cellar door and into a covered wagon.

Sherpa worked her way to the front of the wagon to sit next to Harriet, excited beyond belief to be able to talk with such a historical icon. Just as she mouthed the words "Hello, Mrs. Tubman," she felt a huge jolt. She was no longer in the wagon and felt herself swirling uncontrollably. This time travel experience was dramatically different from other times. Just when she thought she was going to lose her lunch, the swirling stopped and she found herself unceremoniously dumped on her butt—facing Dr. Lichtenstein.

He looked furious, and she quickly figured out that she was in BIG trouble. "Didn't I tell you not to mess around with the RTD?" he practically screamed at her. "You have no idea what had to be done to fix the disaster you created!"

"What are you talking about? Yes, I wanted to meet Harriet Tubman, but I never even spoke with her!" Sherpa exclaimed, trying to defend herself.

Dr. L took a few deep breaths to control himself. "Actually, not only did you speak with Harriet Tubman, but with a lot of other people too. I had to manipulate time to take you back far enough to undo the damage caused."

"I don't understand…" Sherpa said in a confused tone.

"In scientific terms, you inserted yourself as a variable in an existing situation. The variable, you, caused a chain of events that culminated in catastrophe," he angrily spat out.

"English, please."

Dr. Lichtenstein glared at her. "You forced the RTD to take you to a place you weren't needed. Long story short, because of you, the wagon was discovered. Harriet was jailed, contracted influenza from an inmate, and died. As a result, she never completed her legacy. Hundreds of slaves never escaped, and thousands more soldiers died because she was not there to serve as a spy for the Union forces. It changed the historical landscape completely. I can't even begin to tell you how many inventions never happened because people didn't exist to create them!"

Sherpa was shell-shocked. Tears welling in her eyes, she apologized. "I am so sorry! Is everything OK now?"

Relaxing a bit, he said, "Yes. History is back to normal. But you have no idea what it took for us to create algorithms to pull you back in time to find just the right trajectory to get you on the RTD's path. It did create one other bad outcome. We're convinced General Aveel now knows about our time travel."

"I never dreamed…" her voice dropped off. "I assume my mother knows…?" The last thing Sherpa wanted to do was to disappoint her mom and lose out on her dream of becoming chancellor of positivity.

"She knows there was an issue, but I didn't tell her how bad it was. You aren't in trouble—with her."

Relief ran through her body. "Thank you. I promise it won't happen again. No more red buttons for me unless directly related to the mission. I won't let you down again, Dr. Lichtenstein." Sherpa looked around. "Where are we?"

Turning his back on her, he pulled out his RTD. "You are about to start your next hop, and I have to get back to the lab. We lost time with our HuBot research fixing this snafu." After a moment he turned back around, his voice softened, and he looked intently at Sherpa. "If I hadn't been closely monitoring history and the RTD

Notification Program, you would have died too. This isn't a game—you have to be careful, Sherpa. Watch out for Aveel's goons. I don't want to lose you." With that, he pressed the red button, spoke the word "Lab," and disappeared into thin air.

Chapter

Back on Track

SHERPA FELT LIKE CRYING. SHE HATED making mistakes, especially huge ones.

It was great to see Dr. L, but not under those circumstances. And what did he mean by the fact he didn't want to lose her? Could he possibly like her? Or was he just obligated to care due to her world-saving assignment and because her mom was Ruler of the Western World? "UGH, I'm overanalyzing again!" she cried out. "I need to run!"

A quick check of her attire surprised her; she was wearing shorts and a T-shirt, and her curly hair was pulled back in a ponytail. A small backpack held the RTD, some Canadian dollars, her manual, the Instascreen, and a bottle of water. She pulled out the RTD and smiled after reading the display. There was a message saying, "Run, eat, and then press the BLUE button."

Sherpa was not sure what city or year she was in, but it didn't matter. She ran so long she lost track of time. When she finally finished, she felt much better and was incredibly famished. She ordered a huge turkey sandwich, french fries, and a root beer float from a deli she found and leisurely ate while sitting on a park bench overlooking a river. She laughed watching the mallard ducks dive for food and play carefree in the water; it was the most calm she had been since learning about her mission to save the world.

Reluctantly deciding the break should probably end, Sherpa reached into the backpack for the RTD. It was still amazing to watch a circle of metal come to life simply by being in the palm of her hand. Pressing the blue button, she thought, "I really hope I come out bathed."

It was a bit of a shock going from a serene park bench on a sunny day to standing in the middle of a dirty street in the heart of a city. It was pouring rain, and Sherpa ran as fast as her long skirt would let her to the closest building. It was a train station. According to the RTD, the year was 1916, and she was in Chicago. A quick sniff assured her that she indeed was clean. "Good thing, or my next assignment wouldn't have wanted to spend too much time with me!" she thought with relief.

A girl about her age was standing in line to purchase a ticket. "Hmm, she looks really familiar. I know I've seen pictures of her before." Sherpa glanced at the RTD. Immediately she realized why the girl looked familiar. It was Amelia Earhart! "How cool is this job?" Sherpa asked herself—rhetorically, of course. Sherpa quickly jumped in line behind Amelia and listened closely as Amelia told the man behind the ticket counter her destination. Sherpa purchased a ticket to the same location.

In a stroke of good luck, the seat on the bench next to Amelia was open. Sherpa approached her and asked, "May I sit here while we wait for the train?" Amelia motioned for her to sit down and continued reading her high-school science book.

Sherpa didn't need the RTD to see that Amelia was covered with a red glow; she looked really sad. "Here I go," she thought. "Hi, I'm Sherpa. I don't think I've seen you at this station before."

"I'm Amelia. I recently moved here with my mother," the girl replied glumly, looking back at her book.

"If you don't mind me saying, Amelia, you look troubled. Is there anything I can do to help? We Chicagoans are a friendly bunch and like to assist when we can."

"Thanks for the offer, but there is nothing you can do. I'm studying for my high school graduation exams. I thought I'd go to college, but my family really needs the money, so I should just get a job."

When Amelia paused, Sherpa asked, "If you could go to college, what would you want to study?"

"I don't know yet, but I feel there is so much out there, and I want to follow my passion."

Sherpa asked, "So what is your passion?"

Young Amelia smiled. "I'm not entirely sure, but I have a scrapbook full of possibilities."

Sherpa said, "It sounds to me as if you need to keep your opportunities open until you find your passion. And when you do, don't let anything stop you, and definitely don't let anyone say you can't do something because you are a girl!"

Amelia had a determined look in her eyes. "I think you are right. I've been told before that I'm stubborn. That trait may just help me someday."

Just then the conductor announced the impending departure. Amelia gathered her belongings and started walking towards the train. Sherpa glanced at the RTD— Amelia's glow was white again!

"Aren't you coming?" asked Amelia as she noticed Sherpa start to walk toward the exit door.

"Oh, uh I forgot something at home. I'll catch the next train." Then Sherpa felt compelled to add, "I know people are tired of talking about the war, but isn't it amazing to hear about the flying machines? I would do anything to be up in the air zooming around—imagine feeling as if you could touch the stars! Good-bye, Amelia!"

Not wanting to get wet again, Sherpa pressed the RTD as soon as she was out of sight. All she could think was, "I totally wish I could take her on a transport ride back in 2310. Amelia seems really cool. I bet she would have a blast hanging out with Amy and me."

Chapter

Revising the Manual

HOPPING AROUND WITH THE RTD, SHERPA had no way to judge time. She could have been gone two weeks, two months, or two years. Some hops were successful, and some were not. Some were fairly easy, like with Gustave Eiffel, but she had a few really frustrating hops, like with the famous 1960s actress Marilyn Monroe, where nothing she said worked. It was a heck of a ride though. She had met the most remarkable people and really learned a lot about human behavior. The thing that struck her the most was how similar kids were throughout history. As adults they had accomplished huge things and were placed on a pedestal to be admired for centuries. But as kids, they all made mistakes; Sherpa was starting to realize that the smart ones learned from them.

The RTD didn't always connect her with people she learned about in history class. She interacted with a lot of regular folks who happened to be instrumental in the lives of other people. For example, Sherpa helped a girl named Peggy Walters in the early 1800s. Peggy was about to run away to live "in the big city" when Sherpa helped her talk through the reasons that made her want to leave. Peggy decided to stay in her small Kentucky town. She became a midwife, and without her, Abraham Lincoln would have died during childbirth.

The experience had even been fun for her love life. On occasion she had the opportunity to flirt a bit and even engage in a bit of smooching. Why not? The boys were cute and would never remember her anyways, thanks to the failsafe built into the RTD. Who else in history could say she not only helped, but locked lips with, the likes of the teenage Mark Twain, Shakespeare, and Elvis Presley? Too bad she hadn't known them when doing reports in school. Every once in a while she wondered if Dr. Lichtenstein ever knew. In one way, she hoped he did. And maybe, just maybe, he would be a little jealous?

However, after what seemed to be an endless series of hops, she was tired and needed a break. Her brain was on overload from trying to help people when at times she didn't have a clue what to do. Besides, she was also concerned over a potential HuBot sighting back in Liverpool, England during the early 1960s. Everyone was screaming, hugging, and crying at a Beatles concert, but she noticed one blonde woman who just stood to the side and watched people. She showed no emotion, and she didn't react at all when the band members, Paul, John, George, and Ringo, passed by, waving to the screaming masses of teenagers. "That was really odd," thought Sherpa, "because even I got caught up in the frenzy and acted like a total groupie!"

If she saw this woman, or possible hunk of metal again, she would use the RTD phone to contact Dr. L, but she didn't want to call now and appear that she was over-reacting. Sherpa was trying to stay low on the radar screen after the fiasco with wanting to meet Harriet Tubman.

Thankfully, this last hop dropped her off in a quaint log cabin in the mountains. It was in the middle of nowhere, and the only sounds she heard were made by wildlife and the wind. The scenery reminded her a bit of the mountain views from her penthouse apartment back in 2310. It was early fall, and the leaves were starting to turn shades of yellow, orange, and red. It was just beautiful. The days were warm, but there was a chill in the air at night. Sherpa loved lighting a roaring fire in the stone fireplace; after eating s'mores she closed her eyes and listened to the timber crack and pop. The cabin was cozy and had a stash of real books made of paper, and there were some great trails for running. Best of all, the kitchen was stocked with all Sherpa's favorite foods, including a big jar of chocolate chunk cookies.

After a couple days of sleeping until noon, taking long runs, and running bubble baths in the claw-foot tub, Sherpa felt like a new girl. However, she was really starting to miss home and—did she dare say it?—Dr.

Lichtenstein. She would have given ANYTHING to have a slumber party with Amy. She imagined they would spend hours in girl talk dissecting every detail about Dr. L while munching on popcorn and painting their toenails. By the third day, Sherpa was restless. While curled up in a rocking chair on the porch, she pulled the colorful notebook out of her ginormous purple-and-gold purse and reread the material she had written after her initial hops with the RTD. She had been way too busy to update her *How to Fix History and Save the World* manual. Now seemed like a good time. She certainly had enough new experiences.

A big realization for her was that many times, the first impressions she had about people were incorrect. For example, when she initially saw pictures of Marilyn Monroe, she assumed anyone that gorgeous would be loaded with self-confidence. But as a teen, Norma Jean (Marilyn Monroe was her stage name) was very insecure and made bad choices; these bad choices continued into adulthood.

In musing over her time-travel hops, Sherpa determined that her four initial insights were still accurate—she just had more information now to add to them. So Sherpa started writing.

Insight #5: Never underestimate the importance of encouragement.

> ✔ Amelia Earhart: "Don't let anything stop you from achieving your passion."

✔ Peggy Walters: "You can make a difference anywhere!"

Insight #6: Not everyone is open to help or feedback; some people need to find their own way. So you have to respect their choices and just let go.

✔ Marilyn Monroe: She so desperately wanted attention that she would do anything to get it.

After rereading her manual, Sherpa was satisfied she had captured the main points. It also got her thinking about the other elements of time travel.

During her multiple time travel hops, Sherpa "safely" experimented with the different apps on the RTD. One app had the RTD change how she came and left. For example, she could drop in low key without attracting any attention or arrive in a dramatic style to make a point with someone. Her favorite was arriving or departing in the midst of sparkles—it made her feel a bit like the Good Witch from *The Wizard of Oz.*

Feeling more comfortable with the whole "help people be positive and make good decisions" thing, she was eager for the practice hops to end. Sherpa was ready to get to the heart of the assignment and find the right two kids in the twenty-first century.

Chapter

10

Emma and Jose

ELEVEN-AND-A-HALF-YEAR-OLD (GOING ON twelve) Emma Johnson sat on the edge of her twin bed, her blue eyes swelling with tears and staring blankly into a poster of the latest boy band. Her bedroom was painted pink and brown. Emma was not exactly a neat freak; her closet door was permanently stuck open because of all the clothes sprawled on the floor. Her white robe with orange polka dots was slung over the chair, and her desk was piled high with books and papers. Soccer trophies littered her bookshelf. While not considered a natural, Emma pushed herself, trained hard, and was captain of her middle-school soccer team. Emma lived with her mom and twin younger brothers. Her dad lived across town in an apartment with his latest girlfriend. Emma couldn't stand this one and referred to her as "the Diva."

Jose Ramirez lived across the street with his parents and grandmother. He was her best guy friend, practically since birth. Whereas Emma was content wearing layered tank tops, sweatpants rolled down around her hips, and her long, straight, brown hair back in a ponytail, Jose was always following the latest fashion trends. Emma often thought that if Jose would either exercise more or eat less of his *abuela's* famous empanadas, he'd make a great Hollister model. Jose had no interest in team sports; however, he was an accomplished pianist. Some called him a child prodigy, whatever that meant.

Jose's bedroom never had a single thing out of place. Any military general would have been proud — a quarter could bounce off his bed, and his dresser drawers were always organized. Even his closet was arranged first by type of clothing item and then by color. One April Fool's Day, Emma played a practical joke on him; she messed up his bed, rearranged his closet, and separated all his socks. Jose didn't talk to her for a week.

While Emma and Jose may have been total opposites with organizational skills and fashion interest, they were really close friends. No matter what happened, they always had each other's back. One time when they were in preschool, Emma's mother was called to come immediately to the Pineville Preschool director's office. Emma had slugged a kid named Brandon, giving him a bloody nose.

When her mom arrived at the school, the director, Miss Paula, motioned for her to sit down and actually smiled. "I need for the staff to think I'm really upset and you are talking me into allowing Emma to remain a student here. While I am not pleased that Emma resorted to hitting, her reason for hitting Brandon was actually admirable."

Emma's mom looked confused. "What do you mean?"

"As you know, Emma and Jose are inseparable and take care of each other. Brandon is not the nicest child at this school. Despite many warnings by the teachers, Brandon teases Jose unmercifully about his accent. Today Emma had enough. She told Brandon to stop taunting Jose. He wouldn't, and she clocked him. She is a loyal friend. Emma knows hitting is not allowed but did it anyway to stand up for Jose."

As the pair grew up and expanded their circle of friends, they still remained the best of buddies. Their occasional spats would usually end with a flashlight. Emma and Jose developed their own version of Morse code and "spoke" to each other at night from their bedroom windows with dots and dashes of light. Two dots followed by a long dash of the flashlight meant, "Let's play tomorrow!"

Chapter

11

Who Are YOU?

THE DOOR TO EMMA'S ROOM OPENED, AND in walked Jose. "What's up?" he asked. "You didn't answer my texts. And your mom looks as if her head is going to explode. She said you can't come over for Saturday Game Night."

Saturday Game Night at the Ramirez house was an event. Jose had a huge extended family loaded with aunts, uncles, and cousins. On Saturday nights, most gathered together at Jose's house to play board games and feast on his grandmother's famous Mexican dishes; Emma really loved Abuela's desserts. The only time

Emma ever missed Game Night was if her family was on vacation or she was sick. She could play a mean round of Monopoly. The competition was fierce, though; even Jose's normally sweet and demure Aunt Maria became ruthless if she was losing.

Emma looked up. "Jose, don't you ever knock?" Already knowing the answer to be "NO," she continued fuming. "I can't believe it! Just because Madison and I met up with some high school guys at the mall last night, I'm grounded. To make everything worse, mom took away my cell phone, so I can't even text! My life is over! I'm now an unplugged social misfit!" For further drama, Emma added, "I just want to be an adult!"

As soon as the words "I just want to be an adult" left her mouth, sparkles shimmering like glitter appeared throughout her room, and right in the middle of her flower rug was a mini tornado of swirling lights. When the swirling diminished, Emma and Jose stared at the figure of a tall girl with dark, curly, black hair.

On her last swirl, Sherpa caught a look at herself in the mirror. Magenta-colored glasses framed her big blue eyes. She was dressed in skinny jeans and adorned with lots of funky jewelry. "Not a bad look," she thought. Then she asked the shocked kids, "Why would you want to miss out on all the fun of being a kid?"

Emma's mouth hung open, and her fingers started texting, "OMG, OMG" on her non-existent cell phone.

The old-fashioned texting motion totally amused Sherpa, but it also made her miss her communicator even more. "Nice room," she continued. "Like the poster—cute boys, but I still think Clark Gable as a teen was much better looking. He was quite the kisser too." She paused and sighed. "Sorry, just reliving a happy memory."

"Clark who?" asked the still-astonished Emma.

Jose said, "You know the dude from the movie *Gone with the Wind*. My abuela loves the guy. He's been dead for a long time, though. How could you have kissed him? That's gross."

Ignoring Jose for the moment, Sherpa reverted back to her original question. "Anyway, what's up with wanting to be a grown up?"

Emma responded sullenly, "I'm tired of being told what I can and can't do. All the other kids get to stay up late, hang out with whoever they want, and wear whatever they want. By the way, who are YOU?"

"Well, I can tell you what I'm not. I'm not a genie in a bottle—you can't rub me to get wishes. But, all that swirling did throw my back out a little bit—a shoulder massage might get you something!" Sherpa giggled. "Let's just say I'm here to shine a light on a few things that are bugging you."

"Shine a light? What are we supposed to call you, the Spotlight?" Jose smirked.

"You can call me whatever you like, but I'm here for a reason." She glanced up and noticed a motivational poster hanging above Emma's desk with a majestic photo of Mount Everest; underneath was the caption "Aim High—Be Strong." In that instant, Sherpa knew that after a multitude of time travel hops, she was finally in the right place to fulfill her destiny and earn her position as chancellor of positivity.

When Sherpa's hops started taking her to the early twenty-first century, a few times she thought she may have found the right kids. The twins from Omaha were good possibilities, but her gut told her she needed to keep hopping. Fortunately, she trusted her intuition because it had just paid off. This was not another practice hop. The RTD had brought her to the right place in the twenty-first century, and she was finally meeting the two kids who would shape the future of the human race—by ensuring the End of all Wars would indeed happen.

"My name is Sherpa."

Chapter

12

RTDs And Instascreens

"SHERPA? LIKE THE PEOPLE WHO HELP GET climbers to the top of Everest? What a strange name," said Emma.

"Actually, I think it's a pretty cool name," said Sherpa with a twinkle in her eye. "So do you really think so much freedom makes those other kids happy?"

"Duh, yeah!" Emma said, full of attitude.

"Ok, show me how," Sherpa challenged.

"Well, there is this girl at my school named Ryan. Her parents let her stay out as late as she wants, and she gets to go to the mall all the time."

"Hmm," said Sherpa. "Do you really think that makes Ryan happy?"

"Of course!"

While digging through her ginormous purse, Sherpa pulled out the RTD and took a quick peek. The screen informed she was in a city called Pineville in the year 2013 and talking to two kids named Emma and Jose.

"Oooh, is that the latest smart phone?" asked Emma.

"Actually, Emma, it's way better than any smart phone. This is an RTD!" Sherpa said with conviction.

"What's an RTD, and how did you know my name?"

"An RTD is only the coolest electronic device in the cosmos. Actually it hasn't been invented yet. RTD stands for Reality Tracking Device. It lets me see what is really going on with people, what makes up their reality. The RTD just told me that I'm in Pineville with Emma Johnson and Jose Ramirez and the year is 2013."

Jose asked excitedly, "How does it work?" Suddenly his tone changed. "Wait a minute. Are you sure you didn't just Google us?"

Sherpa looked confused. "I'm not sure what a Google is, but this RTD is awesome. You say a person's name, and the display screen shows basically a movie clip of the person's life and what is bothering him or her. The display will also show people's energy as glowing colors."

"Aunt Molly had her aura read before. My dad thinks she's crazy. Does the RTD read auras?" asked Emma.

"Well, something like that. The RTD picks up on the energy field around the person you are watching and assigns it a color to help interpret the situation. The inventor of the RTD developed a simple color scheme, probably because he knew that I can be a bit forgetful," Sherpa said with a sigh. "Anyhoo, people with a white glow are pretty happy. If they have a dark red glow, they are mad, sad, or sick. If they have a gray glow, they are doing something that is not good."

Jose piped up, "In the movies, the dude wearing the black hat is always the bad guy."

Sherpa frowned. "Let's hope we never see a black glow around anyone, or worse, no glow. But if we do, keep your head down and stick close to me."

Sensing the pair was on the skeptical side, Sherpa asked, "Would you like to see the RTD in action? We can use your friend Ryan as a test case."

"Sure, but it will just make me even more jealous than I already am. Everything about her life is great. Even her house always looks perfect!" said Emma. "She's so lucky not to have brothers!"

Jose rolled his eyes. "I'll never understand girls—so much drama."

Sherpa started digging again through her purple-and-gold purse and pulled out what appeared to be a business card.

Jose leaned over and whispered to Emma, "Maybe her card reads Sherpa, The Crazy Chick, and she's pulling out something else that hasn't been invented yet." Emma tried to hide her laugh with a cough.

Sherpa tossed the card into the air. Emma and Jose stared in amazement as the small card transformed into a floating screen about three feet wide by four feet long.

"Awesome, isn't it? It's called an Instascreen. The same scientist who invented the RTD also invented the Instascreen." Sherpa sat on the edge of Emma's bed and spoke the name "Ryan" into the RTD. Instantly a video image of a girl appeared on the Instascreen. Her glow was deep red.

Emma commented suspiciously, "You said that the color red meant sadness or sickness. She sure doesn't look sick. So what does she have to be upset about?"

"Good question, Emma. Let's find out. The RTD shows relevant images to help explain what's going on." Sherpa touched the RTD, and the scene changed to pictures of Ryan's parents, who were always busy working at their family business. Ryan was alone a lot. More images showed Ryan inviting different kids into her house when her parents were at work.

"I don't understand..." said Emma, her voice trailing off.

"One purpose of the RTD is to help you understand that things are not always as they seem. While on the outside Ryan brags about the freedom she has, she really wants her parents to pay more attention to her. She's lonely with her mom and dad gone so much and feels they care more about their work than her. So she's filling her need for attention by doing things. But her choices are not always good ones." Sherpa paused. "Let's back up in time to last week and see if this helps explain things better."

Suddenly the image on the floating screen changed to show a scene from Emma and Jose's recent science class. Pointing to the screen, Sherpa asked, "What do you remember from that class about voids?"

Jose suddenly looked very uncomfortable. Sherpa teased him, "Slept through that one, didn't you? That will teach you not to stay up all night playing video games!"

Emma jumped in, trying to take the attention off her buddy. "A void will always be filled. For example, in class, we learned that when water escapes from one area, it will travel to an area without water. That's how the Grand Canyon was created."

Sherpa nodded approvingly. "Very good! Social scientists, who are scientists who study human behavior, have adapted that concept to explain why people choose to act in certain ways. Any ideas on what that could be?"

Jose tried to redeem himself. "You mean that people will act a certain way to fill a void in their lives?"

"*Exactement*, as my French friends say! Now, how do you think that concept applies to Ryan's situation?"

Jose and Emma gave her a blank look. "Need some help?" asked Sherpa.

As they nodded, Sherpa jumped to her feet. "When people feel that something is missing in their lives, they will try to fill this void. What are some good, positive ways that people fill voids in their life?"

Emma spoke first. "Well, when my younger twin brothers started school full time, my mom missed us not being at home. So she began volunteering, teaching chair yoga at my great-grandma's nursing home. Sometimes she takes me with her."

"Yoga is awesome. I love doing the sun salutation pose but never quite mastered the headstand pose; I look like a rag doll falling down!" Sherpa said, mimicking the rag doll look. "Anyway, now give me an example of filling a void that may not be so positive."

Jose said, "Well, I never thought of it that way before, but there is a kid in my homeroom, Tommy, whose dad died last year. He used to be fun to hang around with, but all he does now is cause trouble. He got caught smoking behind the school last week and will be in detention for a month. I'm sure he misses his dad. Is that why he's acting like a jerk and getting in trouble?"

Sherpa cautioned, "You want to be careful about assuming or judging. Unless we are using the RTD, you'll never know exactly why people act the way they do. Based on your description, it appears that Tommy is having a hard time coping with the loss of his dad and is filling that void with actions that are not positive or healthy—like smoking and getting in trouble. Do you still talk to him?"

"Not anymore. My mom always said to stay away from kids getting in trouble because if I got in trouble at school, she would make it twice as bad at home."

Sherpa nodded. "I completely understand that your mom doesn't want you hanging around troublemakers. But sometimes it's possible to reach out to kids without getting tangled up in the bad stuff."

"How?" asked Jose.

"Actually, it's pretty simple. Ask questions. Before I started my time travel hops, I never realized how powerful questions are," Sherpa said matter of factly.

"I don't get it. You can help people by just asking them questions?" Jose said doubtfully.

"Well, you can't just ask ANY questions. 'Dude, is that a PB and J sandwich?' generally won't get to the heart of the matter. Sometimes asking questions about how someone is feeling or why they are acting a certain way shows that you care."

Sherpa could tell Emma and Jose weren't exactly catching on. "OK, a prime example happened when I spent time with Joe Rosenthal."

More blank stares.

"Joe Rosenthal was the photographer who shot the famous picture of marines hoisting the American flag at Iwo Jima during World War II. That picture became legendary. What most people don't know is that he desperately wanted to join the army as a photographer but was rejected because of his poor eyesight. When I met Joe, I simply recognized his frustration that he couldn't be part of the action and asked how it would be possible to still be part of the war effort. After talking it through, he realized he could still achieve his dream a slightly different way—by joining the Associated Press as a newspaper photographer. And the rest, as they say, is history."

Emma jumped to her feet and crossed her bedroom. "I still don't understand why you are asking us these questions. We're just kids—what are we supposed to do? By the way, you keep talking about all these people as if you personally know them. Most of them are dead, and there is no such thing as time travel. I don't get it."

"Emma, you have a great point. If someone told me I would be meeting these historical figures, I never would have believed it either! It's been pretty wild never knowing which century I'd land in or whom I'd meet or how I'd be dressed." Sherpa grabbed the RTD and pressed a few buttons. "Ohmigosh, speaking of dressing, let me show you some of my fashion faux pas." The Instascreen flashed pictures of Sherpa wearing a futuristic-looking balloon dress from the 2150s, looking downtrodden in peasant garb from the 1700s, posing in a 1920s flapper dress, dancing in a 1950s poodle skirt, and last but not least, styling in a 1980s big-shoulder-pad outfit.

Emma burst out laughing. "With that big hair, you look like my mom's high school graduation picture! Just so you know, the term Ohmigosh is so old fashioned; you really need to say OMG."

Sherpa giggled too. "Wow, I'm from three hundred years in the future, and you are telling me I'm old fashioned. Now that's funny!"

Jose impatiently interrupted. "Sherpa, I couldn't care less about fashion faux pas, big hairdos, or OMG. Is the stuff you've been telling us about actually true? Have you really traveled through time and talked to all sorts of famous people?"

Sherpa put her hands on Jose's shoulders and looked him directly in the eyes. "Yes. As crazy as this all sounds, it's all real. I have met a lot of people, but not when they were the famous adults you've read about or seen in movies. The RTD took me back in time to when they were kids about to make a decision that would change the course of their lives. Sometimes I could help, sometimes I couldn't. But I learned a lot, and now my job is to teach and protect you and Emma while you join me in the next chapter of this adventure."

"Teach us what? Protect us from what? What are you talking about?" asked Emma.

"As far as the protecting part, I don't know exactly what they look like or how many there are. There are some bad guys who have a strong interest in ensuring kids constantly make bad decisions and grow up to be negative adults. I promise to explain more later. In the meantime, let's use the RTD and see how you can help Ryan." Sherpa snapped her fingers, and the Instascreen immediately shrank and flew back into her hand.

"Cool!" exclaimed Jose.

"Is everyone ready to go?" Sherpa asked.

"Do you mean that we are leaving this room using that thing?" Jose asked with both excitement and nervousness in his voice.

"Yes, the RTD can transport all of us—at least I think so!"

"Wait!" Emma fell back on her bed, covering her head with her hands. "I'm grounded and can't go anywhere. If I leave this room, I'll never see my cell phone or have a social life again!"

Sherpa plopped back down next to Emma. "Emma, you are absolutely right. You need to stay put, so let's develop Plan B. Jose, you head over to Ryan's house the old-fashioned way—transporting yourself. Emma and I will wait here."

"What am I supposed to do?" he asked Sherpa.

"Put yourself in Ryan's shoes; you are lonely and trying to find ways to feel better. Let me ask you this: Do you like it when people tell you what to do?"

Looking at Sherpa as if she had three heads Jose replied, "Uh, no! What kid likes anyone telling them what to do?"

"Well then, you'll need to think of a way to help Ryan come up with the best solution to help herself. Don't worry. You'll figure it out."

As Jose reached the door, she added, "By the way, the most successful entrepreneurs get their start by identifying a void and then developing a solution to fill it. I could not get Henry Ford to stop talking after suggesting that horses were not the best mode of transportation to get around. Within a couple years, he launched the

Ford Model T. Henry blew it though; he really needed to offer car colors other than black."

Jose's mouth dropped. "You talked to THE Henry Ford?"

Sherpa winked. "Jose, you better get going."

Chapter

Jose to the Rescue

AS HE PUT ON HIS BIKE HELMET, JOSE mumbled, "What the heck am I supposed to say? 'Hi Ryan. Like Superman, I'm swooping in to save the day because some crazy chick with the coolest electronic toys told Emma and me that because your parents work so much and you are left alone, you are about to make some big mistakes.' Yeah, I'm sure that will go over real well."

Just as he was swinging his leg over the bike, the ring tone of Mozart's *Piano Concerto Number 24 in C*

Minor blared. Reaching for his cell phone, Jose gave his typical greeting. "Talk to me!"

It was Emma. "You need to get over to Ryan's right away. I checked Facebook and saw where Ryan was chatting with Sydney about her parents being gone on an overnight business trip. Sydney told Ryan that her older sister, Sarah, could drive her over, and she'd spend the night."

"I was just headed over there. By the way—how are you calling? I thought your mom had your cell phone?" asked Jose.

"We're using the RTD, and it's really cool! Don't pick your nose because we are watching you on the Instascreen!" Emma teased. "But seriously, Sydney's sister Sarah used to be my babysitter. All she did was talk on her cell phone and chat online. Before my mom fired her, I guilted her into making me a Facebook friend. So I checked Sarah's site, and she's announced that there is a huge party at Ryan's house tonight! Based on the number of likes and comments, a lot of kids are planning to come. You need to warn Ryan!"

Ten minutes later, Jose pulled up in Ryan's driveway on his mountain bike and rang the doorbell.

Ryan answered the door, surprised to see him. "Hey, Jose. What are you doing here?"

"Hi Ryan. I know this is going to sound odd, but do you know you're having a party tonight?"

"How do you know? I'm not really having a party, but Sydney is coming over. We're going to break into my parents' stash of R-rated movies and hang out. No big deal."

"Well, it may be a big deal. Do your parents know?"

Ryan shook her head. "No, they are in New York City for the weekend on business and think I'm staying with my grandma. I told my grandma I was sleeping over at Sydney's. They never check up on my stories. I still don't know why you are here and asking me these questions. Do you like Sydney and want to hang with us tonight?"

"Actually I do kinda like Sydney, but this probably isn't the best time for a 'does she like me too' discussion. I think you need to check her sister Sarah's Facebook page. Everyone seems to know your parents are out of town, and are headed here tonight for a really big party."

Ryan shot him a disbelieving look, went into the house to grab her laptop, and joined him back on the front porch. After scrolling through a couple Facebook pages, she totally panicked. "OMG! My parents will kill me! What am I supposed to do? You've got to help me!" but then quickly added, "I don't want a big party, but I don't want my reputation ruined either."

For the second time that day, Jose muttered, "I will never understand girl drama." He turned on his iPod. "I think better with Bach," he said semi-apologetically as he put in one earbud. Taking charge of the situation, he instructed, "All right, since Sydney's sister Sarah seems to be the chief organizer of your party, you need to text Sydney and tell her the plans changed—you have to go to your grandma's tonight. Make sure Sydney tells Sarah that she doesn't need a ride to your house."

"Good idea. I can tell Sydney that I forgot it was my Aunt Kathy's birthday and it's a mandatory appearance." Ryan started texting. After Sydney texted her back, she gave a sigh of relief. "I think I'm OK!"

"Ryan, you can't stay in the house. What would happen if Sarah's friends still showed up? Can you call your grandma and ask her to pick you up?"

"No way, Jose!"

"Ryan, I know no one likes to be told what to do. But if anyone shows up and you are home, you'll let them in. Based on all the Facebook likes and comments, a ton of people are coming. Your parents will be so ticked off if this party happens. On the upside, maybe your grandma will make cookies. I love my abuela's cookies...."

Ryan just sat there, clearly struggling with what to do.

Jose urged gently, "Ya know, sometimes the best decision is also the hardest one to make. Besides, you won't even have a social life if your parents find out and ground you forever."

While Ryan was on the phone with her grandma, Jose grabbed the laptop and checked Sarah's Facebook page. Closing the laptop with a grin, he said, "Gotta love technology. Party's cancelled. Everyone is meeting at the park instead."

Giving Jose a hug, Ryan said, "Thanks, I owe you one. Now I just need to remember what I told everyone so I don't get caught. Please keep this between us, OK?"

Instead of his usual "No problemo!" and changing the conversation, Jose knew Sherpa's assignment to help Ryan involved more than just fabricating a few lies to cancel a party. "Ryan, we've been friends a long time, and I've noticed that you haven't seemed real happy lately. What's going on?"

That question prompted the floodgates to open for Ryan. "Ever since my parents decided to launch their new business, nothing else matters to them. For a while it was kinda cool being on my own a lot. But now I'm tired of TV and ordering pizza every night. I was spending so much money at the mall they cut back on my allowance. They even showed up late at honors night at school because a meeting ran over and missed seeing me getting my certificate. They tell me the hard work won't last forever...." She added defiantly, "So I'm now running my own life and doing my own thing without them."

"Honestly, I have a huge family that is always together, and there are times I'd love to be by myself, but not to the extreme you are. I'm sorry—that stinks. Have you tried telling your parents how you feel?"

"Yeah, right. Are you kidding? What kid tells her parents to hang around more?" she replied sarcastically.

"Ryan, you need to do something different, or at some point, you'll try to fill the void of loneliness, and it will turn out really bad. Just think of today. What would have happened if a ton of high school kids had shown up at your house?"

"What do you mean *void*?" asked Ryan.

Jose had to think quickly since he couldn't exactly explain his afternoon with Sherpa. "Remember in science class we learned that a void will always be filled? It seems that you are doing things to make yourself feel better, but they may not be the best decisions."

Just then a car pulled into the driveway, and Ryan stood up. "That's my grandma. I'd better go pack a suitcase. I'll think about what you said. See ya Monday."

In the meantime, Emma was pacing in her bedroom, waiting for Jose to return. The RTD had automatically turned off after Jose jumped on his bike to ride back to Emma's house. When Emma questioned why the RTD turned off, Sherpa said, "The RTD has a very specific purpose to help people in a certain situation. It won't invade someone's privacy if not absolutely necessary." She grinned impishly. "So the RTD won't work when you want to spy on your mom while she is shopping for your birthday present."

Finally they could hear footsteps running up the staircase. Jose burst into Emma's room with a huge grin and fist bumped his friend. "I don't know if I can say 'mission accomplished,' but it felt pretty good to help Ryan. Even though I didn't have an RTD in my hand, when I first arrived at her house, I could almost feel the sad red color we saw on the screen. I just wish I knew if our conversation made a difference."

"Well, my guess is that while your conversation today was a great start, there is more that you need to do. I'll be back soon. In the meantime, keep working with Ryan," Sherpa said as she stood up to go.

"Wait!" said Emma. "What are we supposed to do?"

"Really, it's simple. Just put yourself in Ryan's position. How would you want people to treat you? You'll be fine." With a wink and a whirlwind of sparkles, Sherpa was gone.

Chapter

14

Figuring Out What to Do

A WEEK HAD PASSED. EMMA WAS NO LONGER grounded, and Jose had scoured every high-tech gadget site on the Web trying to find a reference to a floating screen or an RTD. He wasn't successful, but not really surprised. They still had no idea who Sherpa was, or where she came from, but there was something about her....

Feeling obligated to follow Sherpa's instruction to help Ryan, the pair decided to spend time with her during the school week. On Monday during lunch, Jose saw Ryan sitting by herself at a picnic table eating a yogurt.

He sat next to her and nudged her shoulder with his. "Hey, Ryan, are we still friends?"

"Hey Jose," she smiled. "Of course. Even though I was kinda ticked off Friday night, I have to admit you were right. When my grandma brought me back Sunday afternoon before my parents got home, I picked up a bunch of empty beer cans in the front yard. It's probably a good thing that Sydney and I weren't there. Sarah is quite the party planner, isn't she? What an idiot." Ryan pulled out a baggie from her lunch bag and handed it to Jose. "Anyway, my grandma doesn't bake, but she bought some yummy sugar cookies from the bakery for me. I thought you might like some."

On Wednesday, Emma invited Ryan over after school to study for their history test and to stay for dinner; Ryan actually seemed happy eating meatloaf and listening to Emma's twin brothers fight over who was the strongest Pokemon character. The girls were studying in Emma's bedroom when Ryan commented on all Emma's soccer trophies. "You were a great goalie when you played a couple years ago. Why don't you play again?" Emma suggested. "Tryouts are in three weeks."

"Do you really think I could make it?" Ryan asked hopefully.

"Oh yeah! Let's get together this weekend. As a forward, I need to practice shots on goal, and you need to practice being a goalie, so we'll be the perfect team!"

At the end of the night when Mrs. Johnson drove her home, Ryan hugged her. "Thanks for dinner, Mrs. J. My parents are usually too busy for family meals. This was actually kinda nice."

On Friday, Jose texted Emma and asked if he should invite Ryan over for Saturday Game Night. To his surprise Emma adamantly refused via a return text. "SGN is 4 me. Not rdy to share. Sry."

Emma arrived at Jose's about an hour before Game Night started. Jose was practicing on his keyboard for an upcoming recital, so Emma flopped on the couch, closed her eyes, and listened. "Jose, I really hope that someday you can get a real piano."

Before he could respond, a familiar voice rang out, "Wow, Jose. Beethoven would be really impressed!"

Emma shot up. "Sherpa, you're back! To be honest, we weren't sure if you were real or we had some bizarre joint dream. We did follow your instructions to help Ryan. Hey, where are the sparkles?"

Sherpa grinned. "You like the sparkles? I'll remember that for next time! I told you I would be back. I would have returned sooner but had a hop that needed a repeat visit. The world would have missed out on some great music if John Lennon had joined the wrong crowd back in Liverpool."

Jose stopped playing and asked incredulously, "You met THE John Lennon, as in the Beatles' John Lennon?"

Sherpa adjusted her magenta glasses. "I did. Loved his accent too! Anyway I'll tell you all about John Lennon once you tell me about Ryan."

Emma and Jose excitedly replayed their attempts over the past week to spend more time with Ryan.

"That's great. I'm really happy you have been good friends to her. But you do realize that the two of you can't fix the situation?"

Jose and Emma went silent, all their animation over helping Ryan suddenly deflated.

Sherpa continued. "As good as your intentions are, who is in control of Ryan's life and Ryan's actions?"

"I get it! Only Ryan can make her own decisions. Then why did you tell us to help her?" asked Jose.

"Because sometimes people need to know they are cared about, or perhaps just need a reminder that lots of choices are available. And certain choices are better than others. It's easier to make good decisions when you have a positive attitude. What you did for Ryan was great, and she still needs your friendship and guidance. Would you like to see the impact you've had so far?"

Anticipating their answer, Sherpa started digging in her ginormous purse for the RTD. She tossed up the Instascreen and spoke Ryan's name, and instantly the trio was observing Ryan having a rare dinner with her parents. The glow around the table was white. They were laughing and having a good time when Ryan took a deep breath and said, "Mom and Dad, I know you've been really busy at the business, and it's important. I'm glad you trust me to be by myself, but I miss you sometimes."

Ryan's mom stopped eating in mid bite and put down her fork. "You look and act so grown up; we assumed you don't need us much anymore. Being busy with work is not an excuse to leave you alone so much. Honey, I am so sorry. I've missed spending time with you too."

Her dad added, "I have an idea: Mom and I have to go back to New York City next weekend. How about you come, and we'll make a mini-vacation around the trip?"

Ryan wiggled in her chair with excitement. "Can we go to the top of the Empire State Building and then do some shopping on Fifth Avenue?"

Sherpa snapped her fingers, and the screen shrank and flew back into her hand. "I'm really proud of the two of you. In spending time with Ryan, you guided some of her thinking to make better decisions. It gave her the courage to be honest with her parents, and hopefully her entire family will be better off because of it." She slapped them a high five." Just like you guys helping Ryan has required several discussions with her, I've needed to spend more time with John Lennon. I've learned a lot lately too. After the first time I helped John, I thought the hop was done. I was shocked when the RTD re-hopped me back to Liverpool. It made me realize just how complicated kids are- me included! Different challenges are always coming up we have to deal with… Anyway, now you have to be wondering what in the heck this is all about and why I've shown up and asked you to help Ryan."

"That's a bit of an understatement," said Emma. "The RTD is really cool and all, but why are you talking to us about it?"

"Well, not to freak you out, but the two of you have a great responsibility involving stopping future wars."

"What?" Emma and Jose said in unison.

"I can't explain everything now, but you both have the ability to change the future of the human race. I'm here to give you the tools to do it and to help protect you from some bad guys in the process. Do you trust me?"

For a long moment, Emma and Jose looked at each other. Jose spoke for the pair. "I don't know why, but we do trust you. But I don't get how or why we are supposed to save the human race. Shouldn't that assignment be given to people with more power, like presidents or prime ministers?"

Sherpa enveloped both kids in a huge hug. "While your names may never show up in the history books, the lives you touch will set off a chain reaction leading to something huge. You may have heard the phrase 'behind every great man is a great woman'? "

Jose nodded. "Yeah, my mom actually tells my dad that a lot."

"Well, in this case, behind world peace are a couple of kids."

Emma looked worried. "Sherpa, are you sure you landed in the right place? Jose and I aren't exactly the female and Hispanic version of Batman and Robin. We're just normal kids."

"Believe me, you are the right ones, and we'll figure this out together." Her voice was much more confident than she really felt. Stomach churning, Sherpa thought, "We have to be successful. There is no choice. The End of all Wars *must* still happen!"

Chapter

15

The Road of Life

"I MENTIONED I HAD SOME TOOLS TO SHARE with you. This one is instrumental to understanding why it is so important for kids to make good decisions." Emma and Jose's eyes almost popped out of their heads as Sherpa pulled from the depths of her purple-and-gold purse what looked to be a long, rectangular piece of silk rolled up to the size of a wrapping paper tube. It contained every color imaginable and was edged in gold more vibrant than King Tut's mask.

Emma breathlessly said, "That is the most beautiful thing I've ever seen!"

Grinning, Sherpa said, "You haven't seen anything yet!" With bracelets jangling, in one fluid motion Sherpa snapped open the silk. Instantly the walls of Jose's basement disappeared, and the three were standing on a road. But this wasn't your average street, it was spectacular. Every few yards, there were silver stars, and the colors of the road changed in large patches as far as the eye could see.

Emma and Jose looked around in awe. The sky was pitch black, yet there were so many twinkling stars that combined with the brightness of the full moon, it seemed as light as day. There was a slight breeze, and the air smelled fresh; like right after a spring rainstorm.

Finally Jose spoke. "Where are we?"

"This is the Road of Life! Each of the silver stars represents a year. As modern medicine advances, I have to keep adding stars—a good problem to have," she added with a giggle. "By the time you are an adult, it is expected that the average lifespan for humans in developed countries will be around ninety-one years. Being an optimist, I've added enough stars to make it an even hundred. I like round numbers—learned that from Madame Marie Curie. I'll let you in on a little secret. By the time 2310 rolls around, life expectancy is around 130 years!"

"I still don't understand," said Jose. "What does all this have to do with us saving humankind?"

"Jolly good query, as my British friends say. It's hard for people to understand conflicting statements like 'Life is short' and'Don't rush it—you have lots of time.' So this beautiful work of art that we are walking on shows firsthand all that happens during the journey of life."

"Huh?"

Sherpa decided to try another tactic to explain. "Emma, when your dad is trying to put together a new toy for your younger brothers that has lots of pieces, what happens?"

"Well, he tries to put it together, swears a few times, and then finally reads the directions. That usually works," said Emma.

"Do the instructions have diagrams or pictures that make the process of putting the toy together easier to understand?" asked Sherpa.

"Yeah, usually."

"Then think of this Road of Life as a diagram that provides the information you need to understand how the choices you make as a kid and the attitude you have will impact your adult life and health," Sherpa said. "If you two can understand this, it will make guiding others much easier."

"That makes sense," said Jose. "Sometimes when my mom barks an order to do something, I don't want to listen. But when she explains the reason why, I may still not want to do it, but at least I understand."

"Great comparison, Jose! In fact, comparisons and analogies are really good ways to help people understand an issue or realize they have more options."

"Let me guess, you used an analogy with George Washington so he wouldn't cut down the cherry tree," Jose remarked dryly.

Sherpa tussled his hair. "I get it, Jose. You are tired of the history lessons. It's just that you are the first people I've been able to share all these cool stories with. Can you imagine meeting Pocahontas and not being able to tell anyone? She was amazing! I'll try to tone it down a bit, but no promises!"

"I guess you have a point," said Emma sympathetically. "I won a radio contest once by being the forty-fourth caller and got to meet my favorite singer when she came to Pineville for a concert. I texted and emailed the picture of us to everyone I knew. There was no way I wasn't telling the entire world!"

"Thanks for understanding, Emma. OK, let's start walking!"

"Why is this area pink and blue?" asked Emma, pointing to the space encompassing the first four stars. "Wait, I get it—babies!"

"Exactly. When you think about it, babies have to learn an amazing number of life fundamentals between birth and four years of age."

"What can babies possibly learn? They're like, babies," said Jose a bit disdainfully.

"Actually, babies have to learn quite a bit, including the critical skills of eating, walking, playing, and understanding rules."

"Oh," Jose replied a bit sheepishly.

As they continued, the road around the stars for ages five to ten changed to the color of freshly cut, green grass. "So Emma, what do you remember most from ages five to ten?" asked Sherpa.

"Well, I met Ryan in kindergarten. We sat next to each other in circle time. I remember learning to read chapter books, doing math tables, and getting dropped off at birthday parties instead of mom staying the whole time. I also had a lot of floods for pants because I grew so much—Mom said to call them capris!"

Sherpa nodded approvingly. "So what you are saying is your focus of growth was physically growing bigger, becoming social, and learning."

"It sounds so important when you put it that way," said Emma, clearly pleased with herself.

"Growing is important! It lays the foundation for your entire life!" Sherpa crowed with gusto.

Jose said, "Guess that gives new meaning to 'eat your fruits and veggies.'"

As they proceeded, the road changed the color of a ripe, sun-drenched orange in a Florida grove. "OK, chickipoos, this is your time frame, ages eleven to sixteen. What is going on in your life right now?" asked Sherpa.

"What doesn't go on is a better question," said Emma dramatically. "Part of me still wants to play Barbies sometimes and be goofy, yet I'm almost a teenager, so I should act grown up, dress as the girls do in the magazines, and be cool so I can hang with the popular kids. Sometimes my girlfriends and I shut the blinds so no one can see us play with toys."

"That sounds totally frustrating. Honestly, I remember feeling the exact same way. Middle school years are the hardest; kids can be so mean. Actually, there was a time when I WAS the mean kid, which I still feel bad about. Anyway, physically, what is changing for girls? Jose, close your ears for a minute."

"I just got my first bra, and sometimes I want to cry for no reason. It's like some days are great, and others totally suck."

"Hormones!" sang out Sherpa. "They hit some girls harder than others. The first Queen Elizabeth breezed right through puberty, but my mom would probably tell you that I had a harder time."

"And just when I thought this day could not get more bizarre," Jose said dryly.

Ignoring the comment, Sherpa asked, "Jose—your turn. What is going on physically with boys your age?"

"My mom said she may take out a home equity loan just to feed me and my cousins. Probably the most embarrassing thing is when my voice changes in mid conversation. We actually talked about this in health class."

"Someday you will be able to laugh about it. Remember, all boys go through it. Anyway," said Sherpa, "is it fair to say that during this time period you both are still physically growing bigger, becoming more social, and learning?"

"Yeah, but it's different than the 'green' time period on the Road of Life. There are now outside pressures that make things more complicated. It was easy when my biggest school decision was PB and J or cheese sandwich. Now I have to navigate the minefields of peer pressure and not being a total loser. Does it get any easier in the next phase?" asked Emma hopefully.

"Keep walking and tell me what you think," said Sherpa. The road around the stars of ages sixteen to twenty-one was various shades of yellow ranging from mustard to lemon. Sherpa asked, "What events typically happen for kids during this time period?"

"Easy answer: lots of awesome stuff. A driver's license, prom, high school graduation, voting, starting college, and legal drinking age!" said Jose enthusiastically.

"You named a lot of big milestone events. Do any of these make you a grown-up?"

Jose whispered to Emma, "Is this a trick question?"

Emma shrugged.

After clearing his throat, he said, "Things like driving, drinking, and going to college are things that adults do, but the act of doing them doesn't necessarily make you a grown-up."

Sparkles flew through the air. "Exactly right!"

"Everything will be so much easier when we're adults," said Emma.

"Why?" asked Sherpa.

"No one tells you what to do. You are in charge of your own destiny. You can live where you want, do what you want, sleep as late as you want, and buy whatever you want. It will totally rock!" Emma yelled out enthusiastically.

"True," agreed Sherpa, "you are in charge of yourself. And you will also be financially responsible for yourself. How will you pay for everything you want?"

"A great job of course," replied Emma indignantly.

"Will your boss let you do what you want, when you want, sleep as late as you want, and still give you a huge paycheck?"

"Yes! I mean no...I'm not sure..."

"The point I'm trying to make," said Sherpa patiently, "is that while each decade or milestone has some fabulous features, there are still responsibilities. Some are fun, and others are a bit more challenging. Here is an example," Sherpa said as she pulled the Instascreen out of her ginormous purse.

Jose looked up at the display, surprised to see his parents lying on the beach during their recent anniversary trip to Mexico. "They look happy," he said.

"Listen to what they are saying," Sherpa said.

"It is so nice sleeping in and not worrying about work. It reminds me a bit of being a kid again—no responsibilities, no one to take care of, no bills to pay—at least until the credit card bill for this vacation arrives," Jose's dad said with a laugh.

"I know," Jose's mom said. "Some days I crave not having to take care of anyone—just for a little while."

Sherpa turned off the RTD.

"That was a shocker," said Jose. "I can't wait to grow up, and they liked being kids."

The three found themselves standing in the middle of the purple decade of the twenties. "What do you see when you look ahead?" asked Sherpa.

"There is a lot of distance from the twenties to the end of the road," Emma observed.

"Now look backward where we just came from. What do you see?"

"The distance is pretty short," said Jose.

Sherpa said, "I don't know about you, but from the time I was born to around age ten, I was either at school or someone was taking care of me all the time."

"So what you are saying is that we really only have from age ten to twenty or so to enjoy just being a kid?" asked Emma.

Sherpa nodded, and another shower of sparkles flew through the air. "I couldn't have said it better myself!"

"One more question, Sherpa. Why do some people make it all the way down the road living a long time and others don't?" asked Jose while brushing sparkles out of his hair.

"Wow, that's a huge question that I don't have the entire answer for. But I can tell you that choices you make now will impact the rest of your life," said Sherpa.

"Guess that is why my Uncle Mark, who is really old, still dances every weekend, but my grandpa died last year of a heart attack because he smoked and was fat," said Emma sadly. "I miss my grandpa. He was fun."

"Those are perfect examples of physical health choices impacting not just us but the people we love. Before my time travel hops, I never understood how the choices I made were connected and impacted other people. Now I know to pay more attention to what I'm doing. Does this all make sense?"

"Yeah, kinda," admitted Jose. "I never thought of life being a journey, but it really is. A lot happens during a lifetime. Some bad, but hopefully most of it good."

All of a sudden the Road of Life disappeared, their feet come out from underneath them, and the trio tumbled to the floor back in Jose's basement.

Chapter

16

The Explanation

SHERPA UNTANGLED HER LONG LEGS, GOT TO her feet, adjusted her magenta glasses, and placed the silk material of the Road of Life back into her ginormous purse. "Hopefully you found that informative!" she said with grin.

"OMG!" said Emma excitedly. That was the coolest thing I have ever done! I have no clue how you did it, but it was awesome!"

Jose walked over to his keyboard, sat down, and started playing a tune. "Man, if I could figure out a way to put the Road of Life to music, it would be an amazing symphony!"

"I agree! But let's get back to Ryan for a moment. The choice you made to be good friends with her had a much bigger positive impact than you realized," Sherpa said while activating the RTD. "This is really cool—I haven't shown you yet all the features of the RTD; it can see into the future. Well, that is, the future for you and the past for me."

She tossed the Instascreen into the air, and the trio observed what appeared to be a corporate board room with huge windows overlooking the skyline of a large city. Participants around the large oval table were listening to a woman talking enthusiastically, and her presentation was dated November 11, 2033!

Emma asked incredulously, "Are we looking at the future? Wait, is that Ryan?"

Sherpa nodded. "Yep. This is a board of directors meeting for a company called AirClean. The founder and president is your friend Ryan. AirClean is ready to announce a huge breakthrough in a product that will clean smog in large cities. That product will start an environmental cleanup that will ultimately improve the lives of billions of people around the planet. Asthma and other respiratory problems will decrease substantially because everyone will breathe clean air."

"Wow! Ryan does this?"

"Yes!" Sherpa replied with sparkles flying. "And the two of you are critical to the success of her company."

"Are you saying I become a chemist, work for Ryan, and invent the cleaning product? I'm really more into music than science," said Jose skeptically.

"I don't have a crystal ball, but I'd say the only chemistry in your future will be during chemistry class your sophomore year of high school," teased Sherpa. "You and Emma were critical to the success of Ryan's company because of what you did last week."

"Sherpa, all we did was be her friend and encourage her to be honest with her parents. Are you saying that resulted in Ryan's becoming president of AirClean?" Emma asked with surprise.

"Well, a lot happens to Ryan between now and 2033, but the short answer is yes. Had you not chosen to intervene and be a friend when she needed it, Ryan was headed down a path of bad decisions that would have negatively impacted her life—and ultimately prevented the planet's air from being cleaned. A lot of things came into play, including her parents paying more attention to her. But none of that would have had a chance to occur without you both starting it."

"Wow. I think now I'm starting to get how you helped all those famous people you met on your time travel hops. What we did for Ryan was pretty simple and didn't take much time, but according to the RTD, it had a huge impact on her life. Could you get Emma and me some RTDs so we can keep practicing when you aren't around?"

"I wish I could. There are only two RTDs in existence, and mine was programmed to allow only me to activate it. See?" Sherpa dropped the RTD into Jose's hand, and the lights turned off.

"Bummer." Jose disappointedly handed the RTD back to Sherpa. "Where is the other one? Maybe we could borrow it for a while?"

"That probably won't work either. The other RTD is in the year 2310 with a brilliant yet gorgeous blond-haired, blue-eyed scientist."

"Is he your boyfriend?" Emma asked.

"Not exactly, but I have to admit I kinda, sorta like him. Want to see a picture?" The Instascreen image instantly changed from the AirClean board room to a picture of Dr. Lichtenstein hangin' ten on his surfboard.

"Oooh, he is so cute! Does he like you too?" Emma asked excitedly.

"Excuse me," interrupted a bored Jose. "We were just talking about the RTD, not some guy who won't even be born for three hundred years."

Sherpa winked at Emma. "I'll tell you more about Dr. L when Jose is not around!"

Her tone then became much more serious. "Jose, you are right. There is a lot more I have to tell you. Emma put it so well; there aren't many years for a kid to be a kid. Now instead of telling you to have fun being a kid, I need the three of us to save the future! There will be times that you'll need to act much wiser than the typical kid. It may seem like some of the conversations you have, or people you help, don't really mean a lot —but everything matters. You just saw the perfect example of that with Ryan's company. Certain actions have the ability to change history."

Jose looked worried. "Sherpa, what are you talking about?"

She replied soberly, "For your own safety, I can't tell you everything right away. Plus, I am still trying to figure a few things out. I do need for you to continue trusting me as this all unfolds. For now, you both need to keep an eye out for people or things that are not right in Pineville."

Sherpa snapped her fingers, and the Instascreen shrank back down. She tucked both it and the RTD back into her purse. "I need to check on a few things and ensure the bad guys are staying at bay. Have fun at Saturday Game Night, and I'll see you soon. I promise!" A shot of sparkles flew through the air, and Sherpa was gone.

"How does she do that?" Jose asked Emma.

"I don't know, but playing charades tonight is going to seem pretty dull after this."

Chapter

17

HuBots in Action

SHERPA HAD NO CLUE WHERE THE RTD HAD hopped her, but instinct told her not to reach for it yet. She was crouched down on a rickety, rusted-out metal walkway overlooking a dark, abandoned warehouse. A quick check of her clothes made her wonder if she was in an old spy movie; she was dressed completely in black, form-fitting athletic gear, and her ginormous purple-and-gold purse had turned into a small black backpack.

Below her, she heard a metal door bang open loudly, and four people entered the warehouse. Even though she had never seen a picture of him, his attire and demeanor made it quite clear who the leader was: General Aveel! A jagged scar on his left cheek ran underneath a black eye patch. "Man, does this guy have a complex. Doesn't he realize that fatigues went out of style over two hundred years ago?" Her attention turned to the three others: one short, bald guy, one tall guy with red hair, and one blonde female. Sherpa immediately recognized the female as the woman she had seen at the Beatles concert back in the early 1960s. "My gut feeling was right about her!" She didn't need the RTD to feel the negative energy or see a black glow; these were some seriously bad people. She bit her lip- hard.

General Aveel barked out, "Status update!"

The short guy, whom Sherpa decided to nickname Baldy, spoke first. "Yes sir. Welcome to the year 2013. The two HuBots here have experimented with time travel over the past century and were mildly successful with causing problems. Our biggest success led to the building of the Berlin Wall. Unfortunately that success only lasted thirty years."

General Aveel was obviously not pleased. "I need our efforts to last three hundred years in order to stop the End of all Wars—thirty years is not good enough! Do I need to replace you as the lead for Operation World Domination?"

Even at a distance, Sherpa could see Baldy start sweating profusely. "No, sir. While we played around with causing problems, the tactic was for the HuBots to download information about human behavior so we can further hone our plan. With all the analysis conducted during our time travel, we've determined that the early twenty-first century has the most potential for good—and the most potential for evil."

A menacing smirk came to General Aveel's face. "Excellent. I fully expect you have a plan to bring out the worst in human behavior."

"Yes sir!" Baldy said. "While adults are certainly capable of doing really bad things, we know kids influence one another even more. So our strategy is to torment a lot of kids, who will grow up to teach their children how to torment others." Baldy gave a sinister laugh. "By the end of three hundred years, there won't be enough peace-loving people to create the End of all Wars. And you, General Aveel, will conquer the world!"

Baldy walked over to the HuBots and ordered, "Transform!" Sherpa couldn't believe her eyes. The female and male HuBots started shrinking. They altered themselves to look like twelve-year-olds! The man-turned-boy HuBot still had red hair but was now dressed in low-riding, torn jeans and a T-shirt. He looked pretty intimidating. The blonde woman-turned-girl HuBot was wearing lots of bling and carrying a designer purse.

Baldy continued talking. "This first pair of HuBots will start infiltrating the schools, parks, and shopping malls. Their mission is to become ringleaders of sorts and train kids to become bullies. We programmed them to stop short of creating gangs; we don't want to draw the attention of local police."

The rock in the pit of her stomach reached epic proportions. Sherpa finally understood the magnitude of what her mother was telling her. If this band of goons achieved their goal, the world as she knew it back in 2310 would cease to exist! "OMG! That's how they are going to do it! They'll use HuBots to create bullies. The bullies will cause kids to become more negative. I've got to get this information to my mother!" Sherpa pulled out the RTD, but nothing happened. No lights, no blinking, no nothing. "Crud! They must have some sort of electro-magnetic shield in this warehouse that prevents the RTD from working." Then her mind quickly shifted back to Baldy's words "first pair."

General Aveel nodded approvingly while Baldy continued describing Operation World Domination. "Back at our Laboratory in 2310, we are in the process of perfecting thousands more HuBots for deployment globally. The biggest hurdles are the many languages, text abbreviations, dialects, and slang that people had in the twenty-first century. But once our scientists figure it out, success is guaranteed! I'm heading back to 2310 tonight to get a progress report."

Sherpa's heart was racing; she was staring into the face of pure evil. Just when things couldn't get any worse, a rusted beam splintered below her right foot, making a loud clatter. The four looked up, shocked to see someone else in the dark warehouse. She was discovered!

Aveel shrieked, "Get him!"

The HuBots took off running at breakneck speed. Their legs must have been designed to work as springs because they jumped fifty feet straight into the air onto the other end of the metal walkway. Sherpa started running as fast as she could away from the HuBots. The instant she felt their strong fingers grab her shoulder, her foot broke through another rusted panel on the walkway. She was falling toward the warehouse floor. Before she lost consciousness, the last thing Sherpa heard was General Aveel's spine-chilling cackle.

Chapter

18

Back at the Lab

WHEN SHERPA STARTED WAKING UP, HER first fuzzy thought was, "Am I dead?" But a familiar voice came through the haze calling her name, and she felt her face being touched.

"Sherpa, sweetheart, please wake up," Lillian pleaded in a frightened voice.

"Mom?" Sherpa struggled to open her eyes. Her body was sore, but not the squashed-like-a-bug sore you'd expect after falling fifty feet onto concrete.

"Welcome back, honey." Lillian breathed a huge sigh of relief. "You are safe in the Medical Wing of the Technology Lab."

Relief at being safe was short lived; remembering General Aveel's plan hit her like a ton of bricks. She struggled to sit up. "Mom, it's worse than you thought!"

"Shh, shh. Just relax, Sherpa. We know everything. Dr. Lichtenstein was able to pull the video and audio of your time in the warehouse off the RTD. General Aveel and his chief deputy confirmed what the Intelligence Agency has picked up through our intelligence sources. Now we even know the code name—Operation World Domination."

"I thought some electromagnetic force field was in play because I couldn't activate the RTD. How did you know I was in trouble?" Sherpa asked weakly. Her head felt as if it were being squeezed by a nutcracker.

Dr. Lichtenstein responded. "Remember when I told you that your RTD would automatically get upgrades when we developed them? When you were at the cabin, I downloaded an app that monitors your pulse, body temperature, and anxiety level. Since all the initial research I conducted on you indicated that you are normally a pretty cool cucumber, I knew instantly something was wrong and activated an algorithm to pull you back quickly. I had no idea just how dire the situation was. Had I waited a second longer…" He grew quiet.

As a kid, Sherpa loved fairy tales and read every version written about Sleeping Beauty. For a split second, she wondered if she closed her eyes, maybe Prince Lichtenstein would awaken her with a kiss. Noticing both Dr. L and her mother staring at her curiously,

Sherpa quickly figured out the big smooch scene wasn't happening. Instead she feebly asked, "Did I hit the ground?"

"Thank goodness, no. Dr. Lichtenstein pulled you back to 2310 when you were about three feet from the floor," her mother said, tremendous relief in her voice.

Sherpa smiled into Dr. L's big blue eyes, feeling the butterflies again in her stomach. "I guess I owe you huge thanks. I'm really way too much of a wimp to have every bone in my body broken. Though if I didn't fall, why does my shoulder hurt so much?"

Wincing as she twisted to get a look, she gasped at the long tear in her black shirt and the blood seeping from a large gash near the top of her shoulder. It must have happened when the HuBots grabbed her!

The medical team robots quickly moved in and cut away the black fabric around her shoulder in order to clean and repair the wound. Sherpa was very grateful for advanced medical technologies as she watched the wound literally start healing itself within a matter of minutes.

Sherpa hoped he'd be more concerned about her shoulder, but Dr. Lichtenstein appeared to forget she was even there; he was focused in on the technology of the kid HuBots. "We've underestimated the physical strength and transfiguration capabilities of Aveel's HuBots. While our Bots are strong, we focused more on intellect, analytical ability, and data-gathering techniques. Evidently, General Aveel created HuBots that are much more sinister than we thought."

Lillian, on the verge of tears, said, "That settles it. Sherpa, you are out of this. I'd rather risk a leak in the

Intelligence Agency than lose my only child. I'm so sorry I put you in this situation. How about I take some time off, and we'll vacation at a beach house for a while?"

"What?" exploded Sherpa with a passion that even surprised herself. "You mean to tell me that after spending the past who knows how long traveling through a gazillion different lifetimes, you just want me to sit on a beach? It is not fair to bench me now! For one thing, I am the only one equipped to work with kids who live three hundred years in the past. This is my life's mission. Plus, I promised Emma and Jose I'd be back, and I don't break promises."

Lillian stood and stared at Sherpa before walking to the back of the Medical Wing. The silence was deafening. The uncomfortable look on Dr. L's face made Sherpa wonder if he would rather walk on a bed of flaming nails than be in the room with her and her mother.

While biting her lip, Sherpa found herself hoping and praying that when her mother turned around, she would not have The Look on her face. The Look didn't happen often, but when it did, fear crept into the hearts of the most courageous of people. The Look meant Lillian had her mind set and nothing would change it. It also usually meant that someone was in really big trouble.

It seemed like forever before Lillian returned to Sherpa's bedside. In contrast to her mother's slow footsteps, Sherpa's heart was beating fast. She had come too far to let go now. To the combined shock and delight of Sherpa, instead of The Look, her mother's gaze was one of both sadness and pride.

Lillian returned to the chair next to Sherpa's bed and squeezed her hand. "Sherpa, you really are growing up. I can't protect you now in the same ways I could when you were a little girl." She smiled wistfully. "The days when Band-Aids fixed everything were so much easier. Yet, if I look at this situation strictly from the viewpoint of being Ruler of the Western World, your impassioned speech is exactly what I'd expect from a future chancellor of positivity."

"Mom, are you saying what I think you are saying?" Sherpa asked hopefully. "Can I go back to 2013?"

"Doing what is right is not always easy. It requires courage and energy to inspire others, even in the face of adversity. You have learned much from your recent adventures. Yes, you have my permission to return to 2013 and continue working with Emma and Jose."

"And about the chancellor of positivity appointment?"

"First things first. We need a strategy to stop Operation World Domination across the time continuum from 2013 to 2310." Sherpa could tell Lillian was in planning mode when she released Sherpa's hand and started pacing the floor. "Dr. Lichtenstein, please toss up an Instascreen."

"Yes, Madame Ruler."

"Thank you. Oh, another request. In case Aveel's spies have infiltrated the Technology Lab, we cannot risk Sherpa's being seen here. Could you please submit an order to the kitchen robots to prepare a meal brought to the Medical Wing, including a big pot of coffee? It's going to be a long night."

"Absolutely. I'm always happy to eat!" When Dr. Lichtenstein reached the doorway, he stopped and turned around. "I understand your caution, Madame Ruler, but I can't imagine any of my scientists turning rogue to work with Aveel."

"I wish I shared your optimism. General Aveel is smart, and unfortunately he will stop at nothing to get what he wants. I ordered extra protection around the Technology Laboratory. While I agree that none of your team may go willingly, General Aveel could resort to kidnapping. And you, Dr. Lichtenstein, are the most critical cog in this wheel. From now on, I do not want you leaving this laboratory unless I personally give you permission."

Despite the high energy level in the room, the day's events caught up with Sherpa. She felt herself get really tired and realized for the first time that the bed was quite comfortable. Yawning, she thought, "I'll just rest my eyes for a few minutes." Several hours later, she awoke in a sweat after an awful nightmare about thousands of HuBots chasing her down the streets of Pineville. She took a deep breath, rubbed her eyes, and reminded herself the nightmare wasn't real. Sitting up, Sherpa announced, "I'm starving!"

Lillian jokingly said, "I'd say good morning, but it is the middle of the night. I recommend eating quickly before the human vacuum, Dr. Lichtenstein, inhales it all. I never realized the eating capacity of a teenage guy."

Dr. L defended himself. "Hey, I surfed for two hours before coming to the lab this morning and jumped right into saving the first daughter. Hmm, good thing I did, since I won't be leaving this lab anytime soon." Winking, he added, "Don't worry, Sherpa, I saved some chocolate for you!"

Lillian kissed her cheek and handed her a bag. "Sweetheart, here are some clothes. Why don't you get cleaned up, and I'll get you something to eat."

Sherpa stepped into the shower, bummed to find out it was not equipped with automated hair grooming capabilities. Wincing when the warm water hit her shoulder, she wondered how long the gash left by the kid Hubot's metal fingers would stay sore. The nightmare still bothered her. "How long has it been since I walked the Road of Life with Emma and Jose? But it's great seeing mom—and Dr. L. I wish I could sneak in a visit with Amy; she would love to hear these stories."

Her grumbling stomach caused the shower to end abruptly; she couldn't remember the last time she had eaten. Sherpa quickly dressed, put some mousse in her curly hair, and rejoined the group.

A huge spread of pizza, salad, sandwiches, fruit, and thankfully dessert, greeted her. She then noticed a fourth person in the room. If Sherpa had looked up "Tall, Dark, and Handsome" in the dictionary, this guy's picture would have been there. Wow, he was hot! Too bad he was so old—he looked at least thirty. She hoped he hadn't been around to notice her pre-shower bed head.

Mr. Tall, Dark, and Handsome was all business and had a grave expression on his face when he shook her hand. "Hello, I am James McNally. I work for your mother."

Lillian said, "James is my intelligence director. I trust him implicitly, and we need his help in developing a strategy to stop Operation World Domination."

Munching on a slice of tofu-and-feta-cheese pizza, Sherpa listened to the small group discuss the facts and figures littering the Instascreen.

James led the discussion. "Let's focus on what we know. General Aveel has thousands of HuBots almost ready to deploy. Our Intelligence Agency will get a spy with a scientific background to infiltrate Aveel's laboratory and attempt to quietly sabotage their research on HuBot communication. We'll do everything we can to mitigate the situation in 2310, but the bulk of the work needs to be done in 2013 by Sherpa. Kids back in the twenty-first century can't get sucked into negativity, bad decisions, and bullying. That will destroy all the work it took to achieve The End of all Wars!"

Sherpa nodded in agreement. While her mother was clearly integral to the final treaty to the End of all Wars, Lillian had imparted to Sherpa the tremendous respect she had for the people involved in starting the peace process. So much effort over the past hundred years had culminated in the End of all Wars. Every single world leader and billions of people on the planet had had to understand the value of world peace and agree to create the Eastern and the Western Worlds. That was no small feat.

Lillian interrupted James. "I'm concerned for my daughter's safety. What can we do besides monitor the RTD twenty-four seven?"

"Mom, remember what General Aveel yelled right before I fell off the catwalk? 'Get HIM!' It was dark, and a black hat covered my hair. They will be looking for a boy, not a girl!"

James said, "She's right; we missed that point. Good catch, Sherpa. The fact that they are on the lookout for a male and not a long-haired female will help us, at least for a short period."

Sherpa grinned smugly, loving the fact that she had caught something the Intelligence Director had missed.

Turning his attention back to the Instascreen, James gave the command "Dictate," and the Instascreen immediately wrote out all his comments and drew corresponding diagrams. "I have a plan. Sherpa needs to go back to 2013 and institute a formal program to teach kids not to bully and to understand the importance of being positive. She can hire people to teach classes and reward kids for doing the right thing, and…"

Dr. Lichtenstein laughed out loud, shook his head, and turned toward Sherpa.

Sherpa rolled her eyes in return, then held both hands up in the universal "stop" sign. "Seriously? Hold on, James. This isn't as simple as training a puppy. Perhaps you are forgetting what it's like to grow up. Kids in 2310 wouldn't respond any better to that plan than kids in 2013. Duh!"

James stared at her in shock that he, the Intelligence Director of the Western World, had just gotten "duhed" by a sixteen-year-old.

Jumping on the chance to share her knowledge about kids from any century, Sherpa continued. "James, no one likes to be dictated what to do, especially kids. We are smart, and most of us know what is right and wrong. There are lots of reasons kids make good and bad decisions. We need to help kids understand why making positive decisions now will impact the rest of their lives. Thanks to the RTD, I've learned that people are so connected and that the decisions I make will ultimately impact a lot of people. I never understood that before the time travel hops."

Sherpa swallowed the last bite of her brownie, handed her plate to a robot, and took charge. "Erase." James's grand scheme was thankfully obliterated from the screen instantaneously. "Before we continue planning my next steps in 2013, I need to understand what I'm up against. Tell me everything the Intelligence Agency knows about General Aveel."

James started to brief the group when Lillian interrupted. All eyes riveted on her serious expression. "I know Alphoneous Aveel very well." A marshmallow dropping on the bamboo floor at that instant would have made a huge clatter. "My husband, Bernard, Alphoneous, and I were like the Three Musketeers at University. We met at the orientation and became instant friends. I convinced them both to join the group Students for the End of all Wars. Alphoneous was an exceptional motivational speaker — and so handsome. Every girl on campus wanted to date him. He had an uncanny ability to get people to believe anything. Bernard used to joke that Alphoneous could sell ice cubes to snowmen."

"I don't get it, Madame Ruler," said Dr. Lichtenstein. "How did General Aveel turn to the bad side? The person you are describing sounds nothing like the Aveel we know and despise."

"Alphoneous was the most ambitious person I've ever met. After graduation, he rose quickly in the movement, yet I noticed subtle changes to his personality over time. Instead of focusing on the goal of world peace, he was advancing himself as a future world leader. Bernard discovered Alphoneous was building an army of dissidents and feeding them poisonous ideas of world dictatorship. This group actually believed Alphoneous when he said that worldwide peace would cause them to lose power. Peace actually gives everyone more power!" Lillian shook her head in disgust. "When Bernard tried to talk Alphoneous out of this horrific scheme, he attacked Bernard and tried to kill him. Bernard never shared all the details, but he said the attack was quite brutal."

Sherpa's gasp was the only noise in the quiet room; everyone looked stunned.

Lillian continued the story. "Bernard was a third-degree karate black belt and defended himself well. In the battle, he gave Alphoneous the scar on his cheek and blinded one eye."

"That explains why Aveel is so ugly," said Dr. L.

"While the scar and eye patch are certainly not attractive, it was the years of hatred and bitterness in Alphoneous's heart that turned his once-handsome face into something so hideous. He wanted power for his own gain. Yet he never learned how much more influential you can be when using power for the benefit of others."

After a pause, James said quietly, "Legend has it that Aveel killed your husband…"

Blinking away tears, Lillian walked to Sherpa and grasped her hand. "No, that legend is false. Up until now, I've been the only person on earth who knew the truth. During the fight with Aveel, Bernard discovered an indestructible hologram that encompassed

Alphoneous's grand scheme to destroy world peace. It turns out he started his devious plan at the university, and the hologram contained years' worth of data, deadly strategy, and who knows what else. Had Alphoneous unleashed the hologram, our world would never have achieved the End of all Wars. In fact, billions of people could have been killed. In order to prevent this from happening, Bernard took the hologram and said good-bye to the two most precious people in his life: his infant daughter, Sherpa, and me. I hope he is still alive and protecting our Earth, but I just do not know. Bernard is a great, great man."

James stood up and addressed the group. "This mission now has two objectives. First we have to stop General Aveel. Second, make it safe for Bernard, First Gentleman of the Western World, to return home."

Chapter 19

Training Emma + Jose

SHERPA AND HER PURPLE-AND-GOLD PURSE returned to 2013 via the RTD and hopped to Emma's bedroom. Fortunately Emma and Jose were still at school, so she had some quiet time to think. Before leaving, Dr. Lichtenstein added an application to the RTD so she could do her journaling either verbally or through thought patterns. Just talking through her issues was a great way to clear her head, almost as good as taking a nice, long run. Her shoulder was still healing from the altercation with the kid HuBots, so running was out for another couple days. She kicked off her shoes, curled up on Emma's bed, activated the RTD, and started rambling.

"Holy cow. Could life possibly be any more complicated? I never knew what happened to my dad. Now I know he really did love Mom and me. The situation is worse than I thought with Aveel; I don't need the RTD to see a black glow around that dude. Dr. L is working on an algorithm to shut them down, but until then, I need to keep an eye out for the kid HuBots. Speaking of Troy Lichtenstein, PhD...UGGG! I totally, completely, officially have a huge crush on him. When he hugged me after finding me crying about my dad, I thought my heart was going to beat right out of my chest! Those blue eyes are amazing. I don't know if it was wishful thinking or he really was bending down to kiss me when we heard footsteps coming our direction. As much time as he spends at the Technology Lab, I don't think he could have a girlfriend unless she worked at the Technology Lab with him...Dr. Cate, maybe? She is really cute. UGG! OK, first things first, Sherpa: save the world, *then* find out if Dr. L has a girlfriend."

The door opened, and a surprised Emma shouted, "You're here! I am so glad to see you!" Emma jumped on Sherpa, sending her magenta glasses flying.

Hugging her back, Sherpa was surprised how glad she was to see Emma. She was an only child and never wanted a little brother or sister. It was kinda weird, but weird in a good way that being with Emma and Jose was like being with family.

"Where have you been the past three days? So much has happened, and we need you and the RTD!" Emma exclaimed as she texted Jose to come over right away.

"You told us to pay close attention to what is going on in Pineville. There are some kids who are being really mean to Jane, a new girl who just moved to our school a couple months ago. I feel so sorry for her. I'm sure Jane has a red glow around her."

"What are they doing?" asked Sherpa while pulling the RTD and Instascreen from her purse. Sure enough, Emma was right. Sadly, the red surrounding Jane matched her eyes, which were bloodshot and puffy from crying.

"Some kids started a cyber attack spreading all these lies about her on Facebook, through IM and text messages. They think they're being cool."

"I think they are being idiots," added Jose, bounding into the bedroom. "Hey, Sherpa."

"Hi, Jose. Emma was filling me in on what's been going on with Jane."

"After learning how simple it was to help Ryan, Emma and I wanted to help Jane. We tried talking to the kids doing this. They told us they are just having fun and for us to shut up or we'll be next. I don't think Jane finds it fun. Those kids are flat-out being bullies," Jose said angrily.

"I'm proud of you guys for trying. It is not always easy to stand up for the right things. I learned one really important thing from one of my time travel hops. Sometimes when you can't change the situation, you have to change how you are reacting to it."

Emma looked confused. "What do you mean? Jane just wants it to stop. I would too."

"I agree that the best outcome is for the bullying to stop. But unfortunately we can't orchestrate life the way that Jose can orchestrate a symphony. There is a quote by a famous author, Charles R. Swindoll, which sums this up pretty well: *'I am convinced that life is 10% what happens to me and 90% of how I react to it.'* In other words, you can't always control what happens to you, but you CAN control how you respond and how you believe in yourself."

"You lost me on that one," said Jose doubtfully.

"That's OK; I have struggled with it too. It is not an easy concept to grasp. This might help," Sherpa said as she pulled out the RTD. "I recently learned the coolest thing: the RTD has been recording the time travel interactions I've had!" She smiled smugly at Jose. "Seeing is believing; now you'll know all my stories are true. Here is a video of an RTD hop back to the late 1960s, when I met the young Miss Oprah Winfrey. She had some really tough things happen to her when she was a kid. Yet she is one of the best examples of people dealing with them and coming out on top. Back in 2310, we still talk about the amazing worldwide impact she had!"

Jose's jaw dropped. "Oprah? My mom is constantly is saying, 'Well, Oprah says…'"

Sherpa tossed up the Instascreen, and the three started watching. Everyone laughed when Sherpa joked, "There were some seriously wild wardrobes back in the 1960s. Don't ya love my bell-bottom plaid pants! I do like my long, straight hair, though. Too bad the RTD didn't hop me to Woodstock. It would have been great to hear all that music!"

The three became quiet when the scene on the Instascreen switched from Sherpa's psychedelic fashion show to a young girl sitting on a park bench on a crisp fall day. The deep-red color around her almost blended into the changing leaves. The 1960s Sherpa walked up to the bench and asked, "May I join you?"

The girl nodded and motioned for Sherpa to sit down.

"Hi, my name is Sherpa. If you don't mind my saying, you look really sad. Sometimes it helps to talk…"

The girl quietly said, "My name is Oprah." With tears in her eyes, she bent over and picked up a leaf. "I just wonder how so many bad things can happen to one person. Some days I just wish I could just shrivel up like one of these dead leaves and blow away in the wind."

The two sat in silence for a moment listening to the birds chirp before Sherpa responded. "I'm sorry. For being so young, it sounds as if you've had to deal with a lot."

Oprah nodded.

"It seems to me that throughout history, it's the people who experienced bad stuff in their lives who are the best ones to help other people."

"How's that?" Oprah asked skeptically.

Sherpa looked intently into young Oprah's big, brown eyes. "Because when bad stuff happens to you, you understand the pain and frustration other people feel when they are dealing with their own issues. The main point is you can't change what happened to you in the past, but you can decide how to react. I see determination and intelligence in your eyes. I have no doubt that you are strong and resilient; you will be very successful IF you let yourself. You can choose your path."

Sherpa paused a moment to let that sink in. "Don't answer now, but just think about these questions: First, imagine that you had the perfect life. How would you act? And second, what is stopping you from acting that way now?"

The Instrascreen suddenly shrank and flew into Sherpa's hand. Emma piped up, "Hey, why did the hop end before the color around her was all white?"

"*Wunderbar* question, as my German friends would say! Some situations can be fixed with a simple conversation. Others are not so easy and take more time. You can tell that the conversation helped her because the color around her become much less red and she seemed more hopeful. It was a good start."

Jose jumped in. "I get it! Instead of feeling sorry for herself, she decided to change her life."

"Exactly! Ooh, hold on, there are two things I learned that need to be added to my manual!" Sherpa pulled the colorful notebook out of her ginormous purse and started writing.

Insight #7: If you can't change the situation, change your mind-set and how you handle what is going on- control what you can.

What to do:

1. Ask the person how they would act if their life were perfect, and encourage them to act that way now. AKA, "Fake it until you make it!"

   ✔ Oprah Winfrey: You can choose the path you want your life to take.

Insight #8: Some situations can't be fixed with one conversation.

What to do:

1. Be patient and figure out the right time to try again.

   ✔ John Lennon: It took several conversations before he realized that hanging out with the wrong crowd would impact any future success as a musician.

Jose patiently waited until Sherpa closed her notebook to ask, "You're writing a manual?"

Sherpa said, "Yep. Since Mom and Dr. L didn't give me a handbook on how to save the world, I needed a way to record what I was learning during my hops. One of these days, it probably makes sense for you guys to read it. Anyway, so what's the plan to help Jane?"

"Well, as a girl, I'm trying to think of how Jane is feeling and how I would want someone to talk to me about it," Emma said. "She is new to the school and may be worried that everyone is part of the cyber attack. I'd want to know who my real friends were—and if I even had any. Jane has the same lunch period as we do. Tomorrow, we should sit with her and let her know she's not alone. Not everyone at Pineville Middle School is a bully."

"Having a bunch of cousins, someone is always getting picked on. But I've learned that when the one getting picked on acts as if it's not bothering them, the group gives up and moves to someone else. Guess they figure it's no fun to bug someone who doesn't care," said Jose. "Maybe I should tell her that. This won't last forever. But I have to admit that when my cousins go too far, I talk with my parents or my aunts."

Sherpa had an ear-to-ear grin on her face. "You guys really get it! I'll meet you at Jose's house after school tomorrow, and you can let me know how it goes with Jane."

Chapter

20

The HuBots Start Infiltrating

SOMETHING WAS NAGGING AT SHERPA. "When I don't follow my gut, I usually get in trouble," she contemplated. "Right now my gut is telling me that something is wrong." The situation was getting too dangerous for Emma and Jose not to know the full story.

Sherpa figured Emma and Jose would be home from school soon, so she flopped on the couch in Jose's basement, and Bentley, the Ramirez family's Cocker Spaniel, licked her cheeks before snuggling in her lap. While petting Bentley's soft, blond fur, Sherpa flipped on the RTD to see what had happened earlier in the day with Jane.

The RTD flashed several images. The first was Emma, Jose, and Jane eating lunch in the cafeteria. Jose said something that made Jane laugh. The color around Jane was white. "Great job, guys!" she thought proudly.

Sherpa could hear the garage door open, and a moment later, Jose bounded down the stairs. "Guess what, Sherpa. We spent time with Jane and think she is starting to feel better! It's a good thing we did. She said her parents were getting ready to pull her out of Pineville Middle and put her in a private school just to get away from the mean kids. She's pretty cool. I don't want her to leave."

Emma was right behind Jose and added, "I found out she was the leading goal scorer on her soccer team at her old school. We need players since most of last year's starters are now in high school. She'll be awesome!" Emma paused, suddenly looking concerned. "What's wrong, Sherpa? You don't seem very happy. Did we do something wrong?"

"No, definitely not; you both did great! I could tell by Jane's glow on the RTD that she is feeling better." Sherpa paused. "I need to be completely honest with you. Remember when I said that there were some bad guys around? Now it's time you hear the entire story."

"Uh, that doesn't sound good," said Jose. "I think we need a snack before this discussion; Abuela made some *deliciouso* enchiladas and cookies."

Emma and Jose ran up to the kitchen, loaded three plates, grabbed some lemonade, and returned to the basement. When Sherpa took a big bite of the enchilada, some cheese and sauce dribbled down her chin. "Mmmm, this is sheer bliss! The Mexican food back in

2310 is good, but not this good. I have to take this recipe back!"

After the three munched down their snack, Sherpa broke the news. "OK, I know this is going to sound like something right out of a movie, but unfortunately it's all true. Because of the risk of impacting the future in a bad way, I need you to promise me that you will never tell anyone else or do anything with the information you are about to learn. I speak from personal experience; I got into big trouble for changing history by meeting Harriet Tubman. It was not good." She shuddered at the memory. "Some rules you just have to follow! So promise?"

Emma and Jose nodded their heads yes. "We promise," they said in unison, but it was clear they had absolutely no idea what they were agreeing to.

Sherpa then proceeded to give a "history of the future" lesson of the major events that took place between 2013 and 2310. Various pictures flashed on the Instascreen like an encyclopedia on steroids.

Emma bubbled over with astonishment. "No more wars is great, but OMG! You have robots to clean your room, and cars have become personal planes! How totally cool! Can we visit? Do you really live on the two hundredth floor of a building with a mother who runs half the world?"

In contrast to Emma's enthusiasm, Sherpa was grim. "I wish you could come to 2310 so I could show you around, but I don't think that is part of the plan. We have some really important things to do here. If we do not succeed, there may not be a 2310." Then she launched into the unbelievable story of General Aveel, the HuBots, and the plan to stop the End of all Wars by breeding negativity among kids.

Jose spoke first. "Sherpa, I don't think you picked the right people to help save the future. It sounds as if you need the FBI or Navy SEALs, or adults like that. We're just kids."

"That's exactly why you are perfect!" said Sherpa, sparkles flying everywhere. "Kids are the future! You know what you want, you know how you want to be treated, and you want to make a difference in this world—to be part of something bigger than yourself. To be totally honest, I asked my mom the same question: Why me? But she had faith in me, just as I have faith in you. We are in this as a team!"

"A team of three against an army of HuBots…" said a doubtful Jose.

"It's not just the three of us. Remember, we have the best of the best twenty-fourth century technology—the RTD! Plus the smartest, cutest scientist in history is on our side. Besides, my mom is making sure the Intelligence Agency is doing everything they can in 2310 to stop General Aveel. The HuBot Army hasn't been unleashed—yet." Sherpa noticed Emma's face was losing color. "Emma, are you OK? Is this information overload?"

"No. Well, I mean, yes, you did just drop three hundred years of history and the fact that the HuBots are trying to take over the world, but I just had a scary thought."

"What?" Sherpa and Jose asked in unison.

"Remember when you told us to keep an eye out for anything in Pineville that didn't seem right? New kids, a brother and sister, started a couple weeks ago and are in our homeroom. Amanda and John fit in really well with the mean kids. I don't feel comfortable around them. In front of the teachers, they suck up and say the right things, but they give me the creeps, and their faces look as if they've had some bad plastic surgery."

"Gut instinct is important, and everything matters, so let's check it out." Sherpa tossed up the Instascreen, and the RTD replayed the lunch scene in the school cafeteria. Something caught Sherpa's attention, and she zoomed into the new kids' table. Gasping, she realized they were not human. John and Amanda were the same HuBots that had transfigured from adults to kids and attacked her in the abandoned warehouse!

Swallowing hard, she said tersely, "Good job, Emma. You were right to be concerned. The brother-sister combo, though not genetically related, may share some of the same sheet metal and circuits. This is not good. Keep watching—we need to figure out our next step and act fast to prevent Aveel from launching his entire army of HuBots."

The trio continued to intently watch the action on the Instascreen. "Jane is such a loser, just like most of the kids at this place!" John sneered while tossing a Tater Tot at a student sitting at the next table over. Everyone at his table laughed. Amanda added, "Hey, our mom and dad are going away for the weekend. Why don't you guys come over Saturday for a party? You don't need to go to that stupid rec center. Just tell your parents that we are working on our history group project. Oh, and bring your laptops and cell phones."

The Instascreen turned off, and the trio sat in stunned silence. Jose finally spoke. "Holy moly! The new kids are HuBots! Here I thought the Terminator was just in the movies. So what do we do?"

Sherpa's mind was whirling. General Aveel was moving fast on Operation World Domination, and she needed to figure out how to stay a step ahead. "Emma and Jose, listen carefully; this is really important. You must be super careful when you are near these HuBots. They are using high-tech osmosis ability to download all the texting definitions and slang off of everyone's phones and social media sites. Turn off your cell phones, and don't use any school computers when they are around. That's how they are getting information about kids. They can't read, so pass good, old-fashioned paper notes to each other if you need to communicate when they are around. Never be alone with either one of them; John and Amanda are programmed by Aveel's scientists to be ruthless. They are also very, very strong." She instinctively put a hand on her shoulder.

"Sherpa, you need to tell your mom and Dr. L!" Emma cried out.

"They know," Sherpa said. "When I became aware of the kid HuBots, Dr. L pulled me back to 2310." Sherpa then briefly described her time in the Technology Laboratory, leaving out the details of the HuBot attack. There was no sense scaring Emma and Jose any more than necessary.

"The intelligence chancellor is getting a really good spy into Aveel's laboratory back in 2310 to sabotage the HuBot programming. In the meantime, we need to do everything we can here in 2013 to stop them. Ohmigosh, I really need your help," Sherpa said.

Without hesitating, Jose stood up. "Friends help friends." He then slicked back his hair with his hands and struck a pose. "Just call me Ramirez, Jose Ramirez. I like my lemonade shaken, not stirred."

It was Sherpa's turn to look confused.

Emma giggled and explained, "I think Jose is getting into the spy thing—like in the James Bond movies."

"So after hearing the whole story, are you in? I won't lie to you; this is dangerous and can alter the fate of all humankind. Will you help me save the future?" asked Sherpa hopefully.

Emma responded by putting out her hand. Jose put his hand on top of Emma's and motioned for Sherpa to add hers to the pile.

"What are you doing with your hands?" asked Sherpa.

Jose replied stoically, "It's a twenty-first century way of saying, "Let's go kick some HuBot butt!"

Chapter

21

The Charity Event

THE SAME NIGHT SHERPA TOLD EMMA AND Jose the entire story about General Aveel's plan, a terrible fire broke out at the Pineville Recreation Center. Over the years, along with a lot of other Pineville kids, Emma and Jose had spent countless hours at the rec center; it was an awesome place. It had a huge swimming pool, three gyms, a workout room, media center, cafe, and lots of classrooms. While the building itself could be repaired, most of the computers, athletic gear, and craft supplies were destroyed. The next day, Pineville's Mayor Flynn came on the news and sadly announced that the insurance money was not enough to replace the contents. The rec center would close.

"Sherpa, it's no coincidence that John and Amanda come to town and the rec center suddenly burns down. I don't have proof, but wouldn't doubt General Aveel and the HuBots set the fire," a fuming Jose spat out. "I overheard John talking to some kids in the locker room after gym class. He was telling them to blow off their karate class at the rec center and come to his house. Without the rec center, a lot of kids won't have a place to hang out."

"Amanda and John are totally taking advantage of the situation and have already started inviting kids over to their house every day after school—and you know they are stirring up more trouble," said an equally upset Emma. "We have to do something."

And "do something" they did. Sherpa couldn't believe how much transpired in one week. Emma and Jose organized a "Save the Rec Center" fundraising carnival to be held at Pineville Park. Over the loudspeaker at school during morning announcements, Emma and Jose made a plea to persuade students to help with the planning. One group of kids worked to get food and prizes donated by parents and local businesses. Another group planned games and had a dunk tank and a bounce house donated, and a third group sold tickets.

The weather cooperated too; it was a perfect Saturday afternoon. The sun was bright, but a slight breeze prevented the day from getting too hot. Tons of people came, and everyone looked as if they were having a great time. The dunk tank raised a huge amount of money when Mr. Golya, the school principal, took the seat. He got really, really wet.

Toward the end of the carnival, Sherpa proudly watched Emma and Jose stand on the stage and present the Mayor Flynn with the amount of money raised—$5,638.00! She took the microphone with a huge grin and said, "This is great! I cannot tell you how pleased I am to accept this money on behalf of the Pineville Recreation Center. I can see that the rec center is important to this community, and as mayor, I will do everything in my power to raise the remaining monies to repair and reopen it." The crowd cheered wildly. The mayor continued, "A special thank you to Emma Johnson and Jose Ramirez for organizing this carnival. This is exactly the type of positive action that our city, our country, and quite frankly, our world need now more than ever. Based on the number of volunteers here today, that positive attitude was quite contagious." She then turned to Emma and Jose and shook their hands. "I hope you will both join me at the ribbon-cutting ceremony when we open the new and improved Pineville Recreation Center."

Sherpa picked up litter as the crowds started to dissipate, wishing a robot were around to help. While dumping a handful of plastic bottles in the recycle bin, she happened to glance up, and what she saw made her stomach do a cartwheel. "Oh no!" A very annoyed-looking General Aveel was pacing around the park, followed by John and Amanda. Her first thought was, "At least he was smart enough to ditch the fatigues." Then her practical side took over. "I can't let him see me. I know he didn't recognize me as the falling stranger in the abandoned warehouse, but he'll definitely recognize me as the daughter of his nemesis who should be in 2310, not 2013!" She quickly ducked behind a large oak tree.

At that moment Mr. Golya happened to walk by, still dripping from his time in the dunk tank. He stopped the trio. "Well, hello, kids! How are you enjoying being at Pineville Middle?" He offered a handshake to General Aveel. "You must be their father. I hear from their teacher that they are fitting in just great."

Aveel quickly went into charming mode; Sherpa could see why her mom had said he was so smooth in college. "Hello, Mr. Golya! Yes, the kids are thrilled. We were so sad to hear about the community center, but we are happy to use our home to entertain kids after school; we all have to do our part."

Sherpa scowled and muttered, "Yeah, right, you are sad—sad you didn't burn the rec center totally to the ground. I've got to warn Emma and Jose and tell them to get out of here." Thinking it was safe, with her back to General Aveel and the kid HuBots, she ran toward the area where she last saw her friends.

Out of nowhere, Amanda and John appeared in front of her. They must have taken one huge jump with their HuBot legs! John spoke first in a monotone voice, "Hello, Sherpa, daughter of Lillian, Ruler of the Western World. So it was you in the warehouse. General Aveel didn't believe our sensors were accurate when we told him our suspicions—he thought you were a human male. He will believe us now."

Dread filled every ounce of her body. Biting her lip, she slowly reached for the RTD in the back pocket of her jeans, thinking, "Come on, Dr. L, I need to get out of here. Please be monitoring me...."

"Let's go!" Amanda roughly grabbed Sherpa's arm, causing the RTD to fall undetected into the grass. "General Aveel will have a lot of questions for you."

Chapter

22

Where Is She?

THE SUN WAS SETTING OVER THE PARK, AND the sky changed from brilliant blues to beautiful shades of pink and orange. The tired but happy Johnson and Ramirez families were heading to their cars; carnival cleanup was complete. The Diva even came to help, much to Emma's surprise. Just before entering the car, Jose noticed several plastic water bottles in the grass and called out, "Be right back!" When he reached down to grab the bottles, his foot kicked a metal circle. Absentmindedly, he put it in his pocket and headed to the car.

The next morning, Emma was awakened at 11:00 a.m. by her twin brothers running around the house pretending they were in a Pokemon battle. Yawning, she threw on a pair of sweats and grabbed some granola bars from the pantry. "Going to Jose's! I'll be home in a while!" she yelled to her mom as she headed out the door and across the street.

Jose was at the kitchen table finishing up his third bowl of cereal. The friends slapped a high five. Mrs. Ramirez put down her coffee mug and gave Emma a huge hug. "I'm so proud of you both; the carnival was fabuloso! Check this out!" She held up the Sunday edition of the *Pineville Press*. The front page sported a picture of Emma and Jose standing next to the mayor with the headline reading, "Kids Make a Difference!"

"Awesome!" Emma exclaimed. "We're famous!"

"Yes, I agree. But now after being so busy helping you both with the carnival, I have an awesomely huge pile of dirty clothes to get to, or Jose won't have any clean underwear for school tomorrow," Mrs. Ramirez teased while walking into the laundry room.

"Mom!" said an annoyed Jose.

Emma giggled and then changed the conversation for Jose's benefit. "I wonder where Sherpa went last night? I thought I spotted her cleaning up toward the end of the carnival, but I never saw her after that."

"She probably got sent on an urgent hop," Jose said tersely, still embarrassed by his mother's underwear comment.

"Well, I'm surprised she left without saying something," Emma said, munching on her granola bar.

Mrs. Ramirez returned to the kitchen looking quite perturbed. "Jose, how many times have I asked you to clean out your pockets before putting your clothes into the hamper?" She placed several items on the table, including a pen, crumpled carnival game tickets, and the round piece of metal he had found in the grass. "These almost got washed."

"Sorry, Mom." Jose said. "I was wiped out last night and forgot."

Emma eyed the metal circle curiously. When Mrs. Ramirez left the kitchen, she reached for it. "Jose, this looks like Sherpa's RTD."

"No, it doesn't," Jose said. "The RTD lights up with different colors and has buttons. This is just a piece of metal." Suddenly Jose jumped back from the table with such force that he fell off his chair. "Holy cow! It just lit up! Cool!"

Emma watched in amazement as the piece of circular metal came to life in the palm of her hand. "OMG! Sherpa said that she and the gorgeous scientist were the only ones who had RTDs. So why is it turning on for me? Remember, when you held it before it didn't do anything!"

Jose shrugged, still very much surprised.

"This has to be Sherpa's, and obviously she can't do her time travel hops without it. Something must have happened to her. Do you think we should ask for help?"

"We can't tell anyone about Sherpa—she'd kill us." Jose warned. "Remember when she made us promise never to talk about the RTD or the future world of 2310? Besides, I'm sure Sherpa is fine. Let's go back to the park and see if she's there looking for it."

"Maybe…but I don't have a good feeling about this," said a clearly shaken Emma. "I think you should hold onto the RTD." When she dropped it into Jose's hand, the lights immediately turned off, and it returned to being a circular piece of metal.

"That was wild," Jose said while gingerly holding the edge of the RTD and dropping it into the pocket of his hoodie.

After putting on their helmets, the two jumped on their bikes and raced to the park. Sherpa was nowhere in sight. In fact, not much was happening—just a few people walking their dogs. "Total change from yesterday when the park was packed with people," Emma said.

The pair walked toward the deflated bounce house that had yet to be picked up. Partially hidden under the base was Sherpa's ginormous purple-and-gold purse. "This can't be good. Emma, you may be right about Sherpa being in trouble. We need a plan—and fast."

Emma picked it up. "Normally I'd never go through someone else's stuff, but maybe there are some clues inside to help us find Sherpa."

They carried the purse to a nearby picnic table. Sitting opposite Jose, Emma opened it and started to empty the contents into the center of the table. Even though the bag was not heavy at all, they stared in amazement at just how much stuff was coming out of it. When the entire table was overflowing with an accumulation of clothes, snacks, hats, jackets, and other assorted objects, Emma reverently placed the purse back upright. "This has got to be the most awesome purse in the universe. It's like a magic hat. Sherpa just has to bring one of these back for me from 2310!" She held up a shirt. "OMG— just feel these fabrics. They are so soft! I totally want to live in the future!"

"That is a lot of stuff. We thought Sherpa traveled light," Jose said with surprise. "OK—so what's important and what is just girly stuff?" Then his inner techno geek added with anticipation, "Are there any other cool gadgets we haven't seen yet?"

Emma poked through the pile. "I don't see the outfit she had on yesterday or her glasses…oh, here's the Road of Life, though!" Carefully she placed the colorful silk road back in the purse, along with the myriad of clothing. Underneath a package of chocolate bars labeled "Most Delicious in the Western World" was the Instascreen. Emma looked Jose in the eye. "It's a no-brainer to say that Sherpa is in trouble. No way would she forget all this stuff."

As Emma tucked the rest of Sherpa's belongings back in the purse, Jose helped himself to one of the chocolate bars. Then he spotted Sherpa's handwritten manual. "Remember when Sherpa told us we should read it sometime? Well, sometime is now." The pair quickly read through the manual.

When they finished, Jose said, "Her insights seem to be the same stuff she is teaching us, like asking questions and inspiring people. I totally agree with her mom's message: 'Things are not always as they seem.' The new kids at school are not human, and our friend who disappeared is from three hundred years in the future. Crazy! We need to keep our eyes open."

After they put everything away in the ginormous purse, Jose put the RTD in the center of the table. Emma made no move to touch it. "Come on, pick it up again. Maybe it was just a freak accident that it activated earlier. Actually, I hope it does turn on. The RTD may be our only hope of finding Sherpa."

Hesitantly, Emma reached for the RTD. As soon as the RTD hit the palm of her hand, it came to life again, just as it had done in Jose's kitchen.

"Sweet," Jose said. "Maybe if we push a few buttons, we'll be able to figure out what's going on."

"Hold on," Emma said, pulling the blinking RTD away from Jose and placing it back on the wooden picnic table. "We have no clue how this thing works. The last thing we need right now is to press a button and end up landing in the middle of a Civil War battlefield, or worse, becoming dinner for a dinosaur." She took a deep breath and continued. "We need to think. In debate class, Mr. Cody always says to first focus on the facts. So far, we know:

"Number one: Sherpa wouldn't leave without saying good-bye, and she wouldn't forget her purse or RTD. Therefore, we can surmise that she has been kidnapped. What we don't know is whether she has been taken back to 2310 or is still somewhere in Pineville.

"Number two: General Aveel and the HuBots are in Pineville and getting serious about breeding negativity, so serious that they burned down the rec center. They must be somehow involved.

"Number three: Since Sherpa's work on making kids positive here in 2013 is supposed to save the world back in 2310; her mom and the hot scientist have to be told she is missing."

While Emma was building her list of facts, Jose picked up the RTD and examined it closely. "Emma, I didn't notice this when the RTD was blinking, but can you see this tiny hole in the side?"

Emma peered closely. "I see it. Do you think it's for some type of a key?"

"What key would be this small?"

The two sat silent, pondering the issue while Jose kept examining the metal. Emma started fiddling with her ponytail and her earrings. As her fingers hit the end of the earring stud, her eyes lit up, and she quickly removed it from her ear. "I'm so glad that I finally talked my mom into letting me get my ears pierced when I turned eleven."

Jose took Emma's earring and carefully inserted the post into the tiny hole on the side of the RTD. It fit! Excitedly the pair waited a few moments for something to happen. Unfortunately the only sounds they heard were birds chirping and a dog barking incessantly at a gray squirrel.

"Come on, this has to work. We have to find Sherpa." Emma grasped the RTD in exasperation. Within seconds, a guy's voice boomed out, "Sherpa! I wondered when you'd figure out how to use the phone application on the RTD. What is going on? Are you OK? I have tons of stuff to tell you."

Emma and Jose were shocked, each excitedly motioning for the other to talk. Finally Emma spoke. "Uh, hi, this is Emma and Jose." Remembering her manners, she added, "May I ask whom we are speaking with?"

"Hey, Emma, hey, Jose! It's nice to finally meet the kids who are helping save our world in 2310. This is Troy Lichtenstein from the Technology Lab. Where is Sherpa? I really need to talk to her."

"Uh, well, that's the problem. Sherpa isn't here. We're actually looking for her," Emma said.

"If Sherpa isn't there, how did you activate the RTD? It's designed just for her," Dr. L asked, clearly confused.

"We haven't a clue, dude. The RTD is just a metal circle when I touch it, but it lights up like a Christmas tree when Emma picks it up." Jose then went on to describe the HuBots' coming to Pineville and all the events leading up to Sherpa's disappearance. "One minute we saw her cleaning up after the carnival, and the next thing we knew, she was gone. We found her purse and the RTD in the grass."

"Her huge purple bag?" asked Dr. L.

"That's the one!" Emma said. "We don't think anything was taken out of it. The Instascreen and her manual were still there."

There was silence for a moment. Then Dr. L spoke in a serious tone, "Emma and Jose, listen very carefully to what I say. I'm going to bring you to the Technology Lab. Emma, I need you to hold the RTD with your right palm and use your left hand to hold Jose's hand. Jose, you hold tightly to Sherpa's purse."

Jose made a face. "Do we have to hold hands? That's gross."

"Just do it, Jose," ordered an exasperated Dr. L.

They grabbed hands while Jose rolled his eyes. "OK, we're ready," said Emma, her voice tinged with both excitement and panic.

The next thing they knew, the kids spiraled wildly into what appeared to be the middle of a black hole. Colored lights flashed psychedelically, and a loud "whirr" noise buzzed in their ears. Just when they had

had enough, the swirling stopped, and they landed hard on their butts.

"Welcome to 2310!" said a tall, blonde guy. "Sorry about the rough landing. I've never pulled two people simultaneously forward in time before; glad you both made it." Jokingly he added, "It would have been a trip if one of you dropped off in the twenty-third century. Those were wild years. Are you guys OK?"

"I'm OK," Emma said while standing up and rubbing her backside. She took one look at Dr. Lichtenstein. "Ooh, you must be the cute scientist that Sherpa told us about. Where are we?"

Blushing, he crossed his arms and bowed in the standard Western World greeting. "I'm Dr. Troy Lichtenstein, and you are in my office in the Technology Laboratory."

"We're really in the future? Can we fly the car planes and play with gadgets?" asked Jose excitedly.

Shaking his head, Dr. L said, "Sorry, Jose, no time. We need to move quickly to get you back to 2013 before anyone realizes you are gone. Altering events in time is a huge risk and can be a bad thing. I promise, though, if you ever come back to 2310, you'll ride in the fastest transports. Plus I'll give you the grand tour of the Technology Lab, including the super secret stuff."

He took the RTD from Emma and placed it on top of a crystal box. "When activated, the RTD records audio, video, and the colors of everything around it. The crystal in this box has the right transponders to analyze and project those images. All right, it's ready. Let's see what happened to our girl." The walls of his office turned into a movie screen with various scenes of Sherpa's recent activities.

While Dr. L scrolled through various clips looking for the day of the carnival, Jose whispered to Emma, "Whoa! When Sherpa is around, NEVER EVER pick your nose or pull out a wedgie."

Upon reviewing the scene with Sherpa clapping and whooping wildly over Mayor Flynn's comments onstage to Emma and Jose, Dr. Lichtenstein said, "Based on Sherpa's smile and the white color all around her, she was pretty proud of you guys. Actually she looks as happy as I do when my Western World Warriors—W3 for short—score a ringer in flying football. So it's clear at this point that she hadn't yet seen the HuBots or General Aveel."

Dr. Lichtenstein's demeanor abruptly changed and his jaw tightened upon watching the scene where the kid HuBots grabbed Sherpa and took her to General Aveel. As they left the park, Aveel stood so close to Sherpa that his black glow clouded over her red color. He hissed into Sherpa's ear, "We have a lot to talk about, my dear."

Dr. L pounded on the arm of his chair. "If Aveel hurts Sherpa, I will kill him!" Taking a deep breath and trying to contain his temper, Dr. Lichtenstein curtly instructed the robot that had silently glided into the room, "Download all the data about these two HuBots and send the file to James at the Intelligence Agency."

Returning his attention to Emma and Jose, he explained, "The Intelligence Agency was successful in getting one of our scientists infiltrated as a spy in the laboratory where Aveel is developing thousands of HuBots to send back in time. This data from the RTD can be used to alter the circuits in the two kid HuBots back in 2013 and essentially render them useless. The best part is Aveel will never know they are not operating correctly. That will buy us some time to get Aveel's laboratory shut down permanently."

"That's good news, but what about Sherpa?" asked a commanding voice from the back of the room.

Dr. Lichtenstein greeted Lillian, who had just entered his spacious office. She must have come straight from an important government function because she was dressed in her formal robes and golden sash. "Madame Ruler, unfortunately the RTD stopped recording after the HuBots took Sherpa from the park."

"We may know where she is..." Emma said quietly.

Lillian turned her attention to Emma and Jose. "Based on the clothes you are wearing, I can tell you are not from 2310. You must be the famous Emma and Jose I've heard so much about from Sherpa. I'm Sherpa's mother, Lillian."

"Wow, we've met the mayor of our town before, but never a ruler. Are we supposed to curtsy or bow or something?" asked Jose.

Lillian seemed amused. "No, that is not necessary. Now, Emma, you said you may know where my daughter has been taken?"

"The two HuBots that took Sherpa are new students at our school. General Aveel is pretending to be their father. They are staying at a house and constantly inviting kids over. I bet they took her there."

"Can you get her out?" asked Lillian. "At this point, you two are my only hope. It would be more dangerous to send our HuBots back in time. Aveel will expect them, and we can't risk Sherpa's being hurt."

"Don't worry, we will find her and get her out of that house," said Jose. "Sherpa is awesome; we won't let anything happen to her."

After hugging Emma and Jose, Lillian looked directly into their eyes. "Please find my daughter. And when you do, tell her I love her and am so proud of her. Also, you both have my undying gratitude for the work you are doing to help kids be positive. If General Aveel succeeds in turning everyone negative, our world in 2310 will cease to exist as we know it—a peaceful society. Just remember, you cannot do this alone. You need to inspire others to join you."

Dr. L said, "The RTD will be a big help in finding Sherpa. I just uploaded Version 4.0 to Sherpa's RTD. You'll know when our spy is successful in compromising the kid HuBots' circuitry; they will have the same energy field colors as humans. Once they glow white, you'll know you are safe. I have a robot here that will give you a crash course in RTD operation. Jose, even though only Emma can activate it, I want you to know everything too."

Jose, although geeked over the opportunity to know the ins and outs of the coolest electronic device in the cosmos, played it cool. "Yeah, sure. Glad to help."

While Emma and Jose were occupied with the robot, Dr. Lichtenstein quietly said to Lillian, "I have no idea how Emma is able to activate and use the RTD. The programming was specifically designed around a section of a double helix in Sherpa's DNA to prevent anyone else from accessing it. I will have someone on my team do some research into how this could have happened. There is something special about Emma. I don't think it was an accident that after all Sherpa's time travel hops, she found Emma."

Lillian nodded in agreement. "I don't know why, but Emma feels and looks familiar to me. Maybe it's her blue eyes. The only two people I know with that exact eye color are Sherpa and my grandmother."

Noticing that the robot had finished the RTD tutorial, they quickly changed the conversation, and Dr. Lichtenstein indicated it was time for Emma and Jose to return to the year 2013.

"Don't forget the purse!" said Lillian, handing over the purple-and-gold bag.

Jose nodded. "We will find her, I promise. Emma and I don't break promises."

As he positioned the pair for their return trip to 2013, Dr. L whispered in Emma's ear, "Does Sherpa really think I'm cute?"

With a big grin, Emma nodded yes. With that, Dr. L activated the RTD, and Emma and Jose returned home to the year 2013.

While her whereabouts were unknown to everyone in 2310, Sherpa knew exactly where she was- trapped in a basement. As she tried wriggling out the ropes binding her to the very uncomfortable wood chair, she thought in despair, "I'm in over my head. I can't do this. I'm going to quit and go back home where I belong, and stay there…" Maybe I could get a position in the Technology Lab where I'll be safe from General Aveel." A moment of panic erupted. "That is if I even survive!"

Chapter

23

Operation Rescue Sherpa

EMMA AND JOSE FOUND THEMSELVES Sitting in the same seats back at the picnic table in the park, as though they never had left. "Returning was easier on the rear end than going to 2310," said Jose. "I think the drop on the office floor left a bruise on my left butt cheek."

Emma giggled upon noticing a shocked look on the face of an elderly man taking a walk. "Poor guy must think he's going crazy; no one is at this table, and the next second two kids are here. OK, it's time to be serious. I think I have a strategy to rescue Sherpa."

"Oh wise one, what is it?" teased Jose.

Ignoring the sarcasm, Emma said, "Since the rec center burned down, the HuBots have invited kids over to their house every day after school. We need to get ourselves invited over. Then we can use the RTD to find and rescue her."

"How will we get invited? After we helped Jane, they must know we aren't interested in hanging out with the bullies."

"Remember, Lillian said that we can't do this alone. Just like lots of kids volunteered with the carnival, we need to find the right ones we can trust to help us." For the next thirty minutes, Emma and Jose continued to plan Sherpa's rescue.

During lunch period on Monday, Emma and Jose sat down at the table with Jane and slyly passed her a handwritten note:

> *Jane—we need your help. Jose and I are going to pretend to be mean to you in order to get invited to the new kids' house. We want to try to stop the mean kids from being bullies. It's not real, but we need for you to pretend that you are sad. We really do like you and will explain more later.*
>
> *Emma*
> *PS—Don't forget about soccer tryouts next week.*

Jane read the note and looked a bit confused, but she nodded yes. Emma winked at Jane before standing up and loudly announcing, "Jane, OMG! I can't believe I wanted to be your friend. Let's go, Jose!"

They grabbed their lunch trays and stood up to move to another table. Jane was a pretty good actress; she did look upset.

The kid HuBots, upon hearing the commotion, looked up and motioned to Emma and Jose to join them. As Emma and Jose put down their trays and started eating, John sneered, "It's about time you realized this school is full of freaks. Why don't you guys come over to our house after school today? We are going to order pizza and try to win a *Guinness Book of World Records* title for the most texts to losers! We've got all of the cell phone numbers and email addresses for the kids at this pathetic school. It will rock!"

"Cool, uh, sounds great. We'll be there," said Jose, trying to sound as if he were looking forward to the experience.

After school, Emma and Jose slowly walked to General Aveel's house. When they were a block away, Emma took the RTD out of her backpack and tucked it safely into the front pocket of her jeans. "I'm glad our plan worked, but will you think I'm a big chicken if I told you I'm really scared?" Emma asked.

"No. Actually I'm glad you said that. I'm nervous too, but this is the only way to rescue Sherpa," said Jose. "So do you remember the plan?"

"Yep. I kept going over it in my mind during math class. I'll probably flunk the quiz tomorrow since I couldn't pay attention. After a few minutes of being in the house, I'll ask where the bathroom is and then use the RTD to see if I can find which room Sherpa is locked in."

"Right. Then I'll see if I can get any more information from the kid HuBots on their next plan to breed negativity. After everyone is busy texting, I'll slip out and join you. As soon as we find Sherpa, the RTD will get the three of us out of the house. Hopefully the HuBots will assume we just left."

As they arrived at the front walkway of the Hubot's house, Emma stopped. "Wait, before you ring the doorbell, let me make sure that the RTD is working." Emma pulled the RTD out of her pocket; it immediately activated, and she gasped at the display. The entire house was mired in a thick, blackish-gray fog. "There is some seriously bad energy in that house, but I bet the splashes of red mean Sherpa is here. I'm sure she is really scared. Let's get in and out quick."

Nodding in agreement, Jose said, "Whoa, it's quite a party." Loud music was booming, and the smell of pepperoni pizza wafted through an open window.

Jose rang the bell, and John opened the door. "Come on in, guys. Grab a slice and get out your cell phones. We're just getting started. If you don't have a cell phone, we have extras from my dad's business." John closed the door behind them.

Emma and Jose stepped through the foyer of the large house and looked around. Emma was startled at the number of people who were in the kitchen and family room. The kitchen island was covered with junk food and bottles of soda pop. "No wonder they want to keep coming back," Jose said hungrily.

Emma whispered, "Focus, Jose—we'll eat later. Thirty kids texting nasty comments can do a lot of damage."

She then noticed Amanda answering the doorbell. At the door was Marina Jenkins, a girl Emma knew from homeroom last year—with her mom. Emma overheard Mrs. Jenkins ask Amanda, "May I speak with your mother? I want to ensure an adult is home."

Amanda smiled brightly. "Of course. I'll go get her." The HuBot partially closed the door and stepped into the study, where she must have assumed she was out of everyone's sight.

Emma tugged on Jose's shirtsleeve. "Look!" Their mouths dropped as they watched the kid HuBot Amanda grow six inches, morph into a different, yet still funky, outfit, and transform into an adult. In fear of being discovered, Emma and Jose quickly turned their backs, pretending to be very interested in a bag of potato chips.

The adult HuBot Amanda returned to the door, welcomed Marina in, and told Mrs. Jenkins, "We have pizza for dinner, and the kids are having a great time. Why don't you plan to pick up Marina around eight p.m.?"

After Marina came into the house, Amanda returned to the study and transformed back into a kid HuBot.

"Let's find Sherpa and get out of here!" whispered Jose. "I know 2310 technology is cool, but these Bots freak me out!"

Nodding, Emma kicked their plan into action by locking herself in the bathroom. She pulled off her backpack and activated the RTD; the display looked like TV screen static when the cable goes out during a bad thunderstorm. "Crud!" she exclaimed as she shook the RTD. That seemed to work. Through the static, Emma could make out an outline of Sherpa bound to a flat-backed chair. Peering into the gray fuzz, Emma could see what appeared to be a hot water tank and furnace in the background. "General Aveel is hiding her in the basement!" Being in spy mode, Emma remembered to flush the toilet and run the water in the sink. After all, this had to look realistic.

She grabbed her backpack and upon exiting the bathroom saw Jose talking to a group of kids. Jose was trying to smile, but she could tell he was very uncomfortable. Emma bobbed her head toward the basement door.

As soon as he could break free, they quickly walked down the staircase into a huge finished basement, complete with a home theater and popcorn maker.

"Wow, this basement is amazing. I'm sure this would have been the location for the party except for the minor detail that a kidnapping victim is locked down here." Emma surveyed the back of the basement and said, "Look for the furnace room."

As they were walking toward a closed door, they heard a creak on the stairs behind them and a voice yelling, "Hey, what are you doing?"

They froze and slowly turned around to face Sam, one of the popular kids known for pushing kids around when teachers weren't looking.

Thinking quickly, Jose pulled Emma into his arms. "Dude, do you mind? We just want a little privacy. It's not often we are someplace with no parents around."

"Sure, do what you need to," replied Sam, rolling his eyes.

"Don't worry, we'll be up soon," Jose said while giving Emma another squeeze.

As soon as Sam disappeared back up the stairs, Jose dropped his arms and grinned. "Learned that trick from a *Mission Impossible* movie! You try that door; I'll try this one!"

The first two doors they opened unfortunately were closets, but they struck it lucky on the third; they found Sherpa sitting uncomfortably in a wooden chair next to the furnace. Both her hands and feet were tied tightly together with rope, and duct tape covered her mouth. Jose closed the door behind them.

Sherpa's first thought was, "Thank goodness they found me!" But her relief was short lived and quickly followed with panic that her friends would be caught and bound just like her.

Jose carefully removed the duct tape and freed Sherpa's hands while Emma reached for the RTD. "OK, Sherpa, we're getting out of here!" With that, Emma pressed the combination of buttons that the robot taught her. Nothing happened. Emma started furiously pressing buttons. Still nothing happened. Just when they thought it couldn't get any worse, they heard footsteps coming back downstairs. Finally Emma hit the right combination, or so she thought.

Sherpa expected them to land in Emma's bedroom or Jose's basement, since those were the only places she had landed in 2013. All three were surprised to find themselves nowhere near Pineville, and based on their surroundings; it was not even the twenty-first century. They were covered in sand and looking up into the face of the Sphinx. Only the nose was intact, and the Sphinx was still under construction. Somehow, they had landed in ancient Egypt, and a bunch of angry-looking men carrying large tools was running toward them. Sherpa grabbed the RTD from Emma. "As much as I want to meet Cleopatra, this is not the time or the place. Grab hands." She enveloped Emma and Jose in her arms, pressed the red button, and commanded, "Jose's house!" In an instant, the hot sand they were sitting in was replaced with beige Berber carpeting in the Ramirez basement. They were safe.

Sherpa hugged her friends, her mind swirling with questions. "Ohmigosh, thank you! How did you find me? How did you get the RTD?" Then she started coughing. "Could I get a drink of water? My throat is so dry. You can imagine General Aveel was not the most accommodating of hosts."

Jose ran up to the kitchen to get some water. Soon he yelled down the stairs, "Come on up! No one is home; everybody went over to my cousin's house, but mom left a pan of lasagna for dinner."

The three sat at the kitchen table with big glasses of milk and plates filled with lasagna. Jose remarked after taking a huge mouthful, "Spy work makes me hungry."

As she took her first bite, Sherpa mused, "Ya know, not everything in 2310 is better. I think society lost a lot of really good food when robot chefs took over. No robot could make lasagna this good."

Over dinner, Jose and Emma filled Sherpa in on everything that had happened from the time Jose found the RTD after the carnival to meeting Dr. Lichtenstein and Lillian in 2310, and ultimately to the scheme to get themselves invited to the HuBot party. Jose finished with, "It's clear that the HuBots are recruiting a lot of kids to do negative things."

Sherpa said, "Wow, what a crazy couple days. How were you able to use the RTD as a phone?"

"That was good teamwork," Jose said proudly. "I saw the tiny hole in the side of the RTD, and Emma figured out her earring could work as a key. Talk about the ultimate in long distance. We talked to someone three hundred years in the future. I wonder what the usage fee for that call cost?" he joked.

"I can't believe you met my mom and Dr. L." Sherpa's cheeks started turning the same color as the sauce in the lasagna. "How was Dr. Lichtenstein? Did he ask about me?"

"Hello! Of course he did. Everyone is totally worried about you," sighed Jose dramatically. "You are supposed to save the world, remember?"

Emma rolled her eyes. "Boys can be so dense. Jose, that's not what she's asking." She turned to Sherpa, grinning like the cat that ate the canary. "I think he likes you. You should have seen how mad he was when he watched the video of the HuBots grabbing you. He also asked me right before we hopped back to Pineville if you really thought he was cute."

Jose was clearly not interested in this line of conversation. "Listen, we don't have much time before Emma has to go home. We have a math quiz tomorrow, and I have homework. Speaking of homework, I see Emma's backpack here, but where is mine?" No one needed to answer; the color completely drained out of his face. "Oh no, I left it in the family room at Aveel's house."

Emma quickly said, "Keep channeling *Mission Impossible*; think like a spy. I'm sure the kid HuBots will bring it to school tomorrow wondering why we disappeared. Tell them I got a text from my mom to get home immediately because I was in trouble for going to a party on a school night. You walked me home but forgot your backpack. Then tell him how awesome it was sending text pages to 'the losers.' Hopefully they'll forget all about the backpack and won't link us to Sherpa's disappearing from their basement."

Sherpa crinkled her brow. "I guess it's good that you are so innovative. Anyway, it's been a long couple days for all of us. I need to sleep- and think hard whether I can keep doing this" Her voice trailed off.

Emma put her hand on Sherpa's shoulder. "Sherpa, don't quit. You can't let General Aveel win. Besides, you aren't doing this alone, you have us! And we have totally leveled up on this stuff! Oh, don't forget your purse. Your mom wanted us to tell you that she put some stuff in it." Emma handed over the purple-and-gold bag. "By the way, you have to get me one of these! My dad could never yell at me again for over packing during our nights at his apartment."

Sherpa took the ginormous purse and gave them one last hug. "I don't know how to thank you guys. You risked your lives to rescue me. You both are my heroes... and wow, you have leveled up in a big way. You are becoming pros at this saving the world stuff!"

Jose proudly puffed out his chest but tried to act nonchalant. "No big deal; that's what friends are for."

She turned towards Emma. "I'll think about what you said, I promise." Pressing the RTD, she disappeared, without any sparkles.

Jose looked worried, but Emma spoke semi-confidently. "She'll be back, at least I really hope..."

Chapter

24

Taking Back Control

EMMA ARRIVED EARLY AT SCHOOL TUESDAY morning, hoping to catch Jane. Jane's dad always dropped her off fifteen minutes before the first bell rang on his way to work. "Hey, Jane!" Emma called out as she jogged up the sidewalk.

"Hi Emma," Jane yawned. "School starts WAY too early."

"Totally agree." Emma yawned in commiseration. "I'm sorry about yesterday in the cafeteria. I hope you know that we really are friends, and what I wrote in the note was true. Jose and I are just trying to figure out what the bullies are up to."

Jane got a disgusted look on her face as they sat down on a bench and dropped their backpacks to the ground with a thud. "I can tell you what the bullies are up to. Last night I got some really nasty text messages and IMs. But I wasn't the only one."

Jane went on to describe how a bunch of kids were working on their group history projects at the Pineville Public Library the previous night. All the cell phones constantly buzzed, announcing new texts. "It was bad in the beginning. One girl even started crying."

Emma rubbed her scalp. "This all gives me such a headache. The new brother-sister combo hosted a texting party last night, complete with pizza and extra cell phones. I have no idea how they got everyone's phone number and email address, but they did, and at least thirty kids texted nasty messages until their thumbs cramped up. I don't know what to do next. How do we stop them?"

"Did you know any of the kids at the party?" Jane asked.

"Yeah, I knew most of them. I was really surprised that some would even want to be there. I've grown up with a lot of these kids and thought most of them were pretty nice. I never thought they could be that mean."

Jane was silent for a moment. "We move around a lot because my dad is in the military. This is my third school, and I can tell you that some kids will suddenly act different in order to hang with the popular crowd."

"Even when the cool kids are acting like idiots and being bullies?" Emma asked in disbelief.

"Yeah, unfortunately. Hey, I have an idea. Last night at the library, when the nasty text messages and IMs started, the first ones getting them were really upset. When kids saw the majority of us got them, everyone got mad instead." Jane's face lit up. "Emma, there is power in numbers, and I say we take back our school!"

"You're right. Their plan to be negative may just backfire. I've got to talk to Jose." First bell rang, causing Emma and Jane to reluctantly end their discussion and join the sea of backpacks entering the front door of Pineville Middle School.

A few minutes later, Jose entered homeroom carrying his newly reclaimed green backpack and looking anxious.

"What's wrong? Did the Bots guess we had anything to do with Sherpa's rescue?" asked Emma.

"Not exactly. John handed me the backpack and asked where we went last night. I told him the story we made up about you getting in trouble and needing to go home fast. I swear that Amanda was looking me up and down like a robot lie detector. Maybe I'm paranoid, but I've never been so happy to hear second bell. For our sake and Sherpa's, we don't want them to connect all of us together. At least not yet. By the way, what will happen if Sherpa doesn't come back? She was pretty freaked out about getting kidnapped."

Emma then started to share Jane's revelation about taking back the school when Ms. Timmons, the homeroom teacher, gave her the "stop talking or you'll get detention" warning look.

Meanwhile, Sherpa was reluctantly rolling out of a very comfy bed. She slept like a rock. The RTD hopped her back to the cabin in the woods she loved so much. Knowing she couldn't exercise with a full stomach, she figured she had better get her run in before eating breakfast. She needed to think about whether her next hop should be the final hop returning back home. Reaching inside her purse, Sherpa was pleasantly surprised to pull out a new pair of running shoes and a very cute workout outfit. "Way to go, Mom. You came through again!"

She stepped outside on the porch; while stretching out, she took in the gorgeous mountain views. A hawk soaring magnificently in the sky caught her eye. "Why can't all of 2013 be this peaceful?" she asked herself wistfully. During the first part of her run, Sherpa felt the grogginess fade away and her muscles loosen up. She had no idea how long she had been tied to the chair in General Aveel's basement, but she still had marks on her wrists and ankles from the ropes. On the second half of the run, with her mind much clearer, Sherpa strained to remember every detail she could from her captivity, especially the discussions that had taken place between General Aveel, Amanda, and John when they thought she was asleep.

She was also confused about General Aveel. "Several times I caught him looking at me, almost as though he cared. Did I really hear him right when he said, 'She may not look much like Lillian, but Sherpa sure reminds me of Lillian back in university days—they have the same idealism, spirit, and determination. Lillian was special...' But then he got really gruff again and said, 'But I can't risk underestimating this girl.' I wonder if he had a crush on my mom. But the only guy she loved was my dad. Aveel is right about a couple things: my mom is special, and underestimating me is a big mistake!"

It never ceased to surprise Sherpa how fast time flew by when she ran. She looked ahead and saw her cozy log cabin in the distance, a welcoming view with its plume of gray, wispy smoke floating out the stone chimney.

After a long shower, Sherpa was more determined than ever. And she was starving. She got dressed and made herself a bowl of cereal and, of course, a big mug of hot chocolate. A major revelation hit Sherpa as she took the first sip. "When they thought I was sleeping, the kid Hubots and Aveel talked about 'converting' kids to becoming negative as being a permanent thing. As though once converted, kids could never change back. They don't understand that even though kids make mistakes, most of us will ultimately do the right thing. Ohmigosh—that will help us!"

With her tummy pleasantly full, Sherpa pulled out the manual with its always-sharp pencil and curled up in the rocking chair on the porch. She opened the notebook and was surprised to see a new entry in her mother's beautiful handwriting:

Sweetheart,

We are doing everything possible in 2310 to assist you, but ultimately your success in guiding kids to be positive is the critical element in the strategy to defeat Operation World Domination. Help may come from sources you least expect; keep your eyes and mind open. I have no doubt that my future chancellor of positivity will prevail. Please be careful, and I hope to have you home soon.

I Love you,
Mom

Frustrated, Sherpa yelled at the notebook, "Mom, why do you always have to talk in code? Just tell me what I need to do and who will help me!" After an exaggerated sigh, she settled down and reread her earlier entries to ensure they were still relevant. Then she proceeded to write down some new observations.

Insight #9: People change all the time—for the better or the worse.

What to do:

- ❖ Don't give up on kids; simply because they are swayed in a certain direction for a period of time, it does not mean they will act that way forever.

- ❖ Share information that helps people make good decisions.

- ❖ Understand that everyone thinks differently and has different life experiences and different goals.

- ❖ Whether we know about it or not, all people have stuff going on in their lives that directly impacts how they act.

❖ Be willing to forgive, regain friendships, and move forward.

    ✔ Amy: As best friends, we were inseparable for years, but for a while, I started hanging with another group of kids and blowing her off. Her feelings were hurt, but she let me know I would always be her friend. After a couple weeks, I apologized, and we were good again.

Sherpa closed the manual, pleased that she could add a personal example not related to her time travel hops with the RTD. "This insight may be exactly what we need right now. If we can convince kids that being negative and bullying is not right, we'll reduce the size of Aveels's army of human kids and ultimately defeat him. If anyone can do this, it's Emma and Jose. Emma's good; she convinced me not to go back home." Sherpa checked her timekeeping device; she had better move fast. School had just ended, and it was time meet her friends.

Emma returned home after school to drop off her backpack before meeting Sherpa over at Jose's house. They had a lot to talk about. Emma was so focused that while running down the steps, she didn't even notice her mom standing on the landing and almost ran her over.

Mrs. Johnson steadied Emma. "Sweetie, you look a thousand miles away. What is going on?"

"Sorry, Mom. I guess my mind is somewhere else."

"I can tell you are in a hurry, but do you have ten minutes to talk? The house is quiet since your brothers are still at school. It's always chaos when they are around. I took a break from working and made some cookies that are still warm—oatmeal chocolate chip, your favorite."

"Yum...I am a little hungry," Emma said as she sat down at the kitchen table, savoring the smell of the cookies. "It's been crazy at school. There are some new kids who are really mean and seem to be egging on other kids to be bullies too. It's not right, and we are trying to fix it."

Mrs. Johnson placed a glass of cold milk and a plate of warm cookies in front of Emma. Sitting down, she asked, "I assume by 'we' you are talking about Jose?"

"Of course, and another girl named Jane. She said today that we needed to take back our school. She's right."

Gently brushing Emma's bangs out of her eyes, Mrs. Johnson said, "Ever since you were a little girl, you have had such determination to achieve your goals. Once your mind is made up, there is no stopping you. As young as age three, you walked with your head held high and possessed such self-confidence. I really believe that this is the reason other kids rarely mess with you. I'm proud of you for wanting to take a stand. Just be careful and know that both your dad and I are here to help. We may not understand everything, but we fully support you."

Emma was surprised to feel tears spring to her eyes. Hugging her mom, she said, "Thanks. I love you, Mom. Can I take some of these cookies over to Jose's?"

Four and a half minutes later, she was sitting on the couch in the Ramirez basement passing the container of cookies to Jose. Excitedly, she relayed her before-school conversation with Jane, ending with, "Jane is totally right; it's time to take back our school."

Before he could respond, a burst of sparkles announced the return of Sherpa. She grinned at her friends. "I'm back! Thanks for having more confidence in me than I had in myself."

With his mouth stuffed with cookie, Jose replied, "That's what friends are for. Now, do you have a plan?"

Sherpa playfully gave Jose a noogie on the top of his head. "You mean do WE have a plan. But yes, I have some thoughts. First, though, remind me what Dr. L said about the RTD upgrades. I was so tired last night after you rescued me; I'm sure I missed some things."

Jose, always up for talking technology, launched into a commentary of the attributes of RTD Version 4.0. "The thing that will help us the most is seeing the energy colors of the HuBots. Once the spy who infiltrates Aveel's laboratory is able to change their circuits, the colors will change from black to white. Hey, just like in the old cowboy movies—in the end, the guys in the white hats always defeat the bad guys in the black hats!"

Sherpa grabbed the Instascreen out of her purse and tossed it into the air. "Speaking of the Bots, let's check out what John and Amanda are up to right now." The scene flashed to the entrance to Pineville Middle School, where the kid HuBots were in the process of setting up the next "texting party" for the following day, and from what they could tell, a lot of kids were coming. "They are still mired in black, so nothing has changed yet," Sherpa said disappointedly. "But on the upside, it doesn't appear they have changed tactics. They are still focused on cyber-bullying."

"Yeah, but don't forget, they still throw food at kids in the cafeteria," said Emma disdainfully. Earlier in the day, she had followed Maggie Chen into the restroom and helped get mashed potatoes out of her hair.

"I can't help much with the food throwing since it would be dangerous for all three of us if I showed up in the cafeteria; John and Amanda would recognize me in a heartbeat. So let's focus on the text messages and emails for a moment. How do we stop them from hurting kids?" As Sherpa asked the question, the Instascreen became a voice-activated whiteboard.

Jose and Emma eagerly brainstormed suggestions, in part because they were developing a solution, but mainly because it was so cool to watch their words written automatically by the Instascreen. At the end of five minutes, they had a pretty impressive list.

How to Make Cyber Attacks Worthless

❖ Tell your parents or other adults, and most importantly, your friends that it is happening.

❖ Reply with surprising remarks or jokes like "Thank you! I agree!"

❖ There is power in numbers—make friends with kids who are also getting the texts / emails / IMs.

❖ Step in and support kids who are getting bullied- both in person and Cybersupporting.

- ❖ Show confidence- do not let the bullies know that it bothers you.

- ❖ Delete messages without reading- why ruin a good day!

- ❖ When the attack is happening, turn off the cell phones and don't log into email or IM.

- ❖ Know that you are an awesome person and it doesn't matter what bullies think.

- ❖ Report bullying to the school—in writing.

- ❖ Feel sorry for the bullies; they can't be very happy people if they resort to attacking others.

"Bem Feito—as my Portuguese friends would say!" said Sherpa admiringly. "Come to think if it, I'll have to add this list to my manual. OK, let's come up with a plan using the ideas you've developed. We know the next texting party is tomorrow after school, so we need to act fast."

"What if we had our own party at the same time?" asked Jose.

Emma jumped on the idea. "Yeah, but invited a ton of people and made it more like a pep rally?"

"What's a pep rally?" Sherpa asked, unfamiliar with the term.

"Whenever we have a pep rally at school, it's usually to root for a sports team or big school event. There are lots of signs and some music, and it's loud. Everyone cheers for the same thing."

"I like it. A pep rally sounds like the celebration we have before flying football games. My favorite team is the Western World Warriors. Hey, I even have some paper in my purse to make signs." Sherpa pulled at least thirty huge pieces of cardboard from her ginormous purse. "I also have these special markers; they change to whatever color you tell it. Watch out for chartreuse, though; it never comes out right."

"Cool!" sang out Emma. "I wish I could use these in art class."

"Remember, they are from 2310 and for your use only," warned Sherpa. "So what else do we need? You mentioned music?"

"Hey, if it's music, I'm your guy," said Jose. He strutted over to his keyboard and played the refrain from the song "Don't Stop Believing." "I can bring my keyboard and MP3 player. But we're forgetting the most important things. Who will come, and where will the pep rally be held?"

Sherpa's eyes twinkled. "Didn't you two just host a spectacular event at the park that had media coverage? If I recall correctly, you are now close and personal friends of the mayor. Plus, I'm sure if you made a couple phone calls about the purpose of the pep rally, you could get the newspaper to advertise the 'Stop the Bullying: Rally in the Park.' Hmm, I like that name."

Emma said, "I do too—Stop the Bullying: Rally in the Park." She went into organization mode. "Let's divide and conquer. Jose, you call the reporter who put us on the front page of the newspaper. Tell him that we are taking back our school from bullies and need him to write a story. My dad is in the same golf league with the mayor's husband, so I'll ask him to call their house tonight. The biggest advertising, though, has to be at school tomorrow. How do we notify everyone else that it starts at 4:00 p.m.?"

"Easy," Jose said. "Let's announce it on the loud-speaker at school, just as we did for the fundraiser carnival."

"I wouldn't do that if I were you," said Sherpa. "If Aveel gets wind of this, the HuBots could try to shut down the rally. Remember, HuBots can only understand electronic messages, so plaster handwritten signs around the school."

Nodding in agreement, Jose said, "You're right. Word of mouth and signs only."

"Great. Sounds as if you have all the plans in motion. I'll meet you after school tomorrow in the park. I'll be wearing a big hat and different glasses just in case the HuBots happen to come by. That way they won't recognize me again visually. I'll configure the RTD to put a radio wave around me to alter their circuits. Good luck. I'll see you there." With that, Sherpa activated the RTD and disappeared, leaving behind a shower of sparkles.

Chapter

25

Stop the Bullying: Rally at the Park

BETWEEN TUESDAY NIGHT AND LUNCH period on Wednesday, Jose, Emma, and Jane asked the captain of every club, band, and sports team to help get out the information about Stop the Bullying: Rally in the Park. They were surprised at the excitement kids showed. Apparently more kids had been subjected to the bullying than anyone realized.

By 3:45 p.m., the park was packed with kids holding signs like "You Can Text, but We Don't Care!" "Taking Back our School," and "Down with Bullies." Festivity was in the air. On the stage Jose played his keyboard and was joined by two guys playing guitars and Jane on the saxophone. The quartet was rocking the place! A reporter was busy snapping pictures of the crowd and the band. A vendor with a red pull-cart mingled among the crowd selling popcorn, popsicles, and ice cream sandwiches. Some parents chatted in the background.

At 4:00 p.m. sharp, Jose called Emma to the stage. Standing in front of the microphone, she held up her cell phone and spoke to the crowd. "Right now, a bunch of kids are starting to send text pages, IMs, and emails to us, the supposed 'losers' of Pineville Middle School. But I'm looking around, and there are a lot of really cool kids here. There are absolutely NO losers standing in this park!" With that the crowd went crazy. She continued, her voice growing louder and more confident. "Words cannot hurt us if we don't let them! There is power in numbers. If we ignore the bullies and focus on one another, they can't hurt us. And maybe, just maybe, they will decide it's easier to just be our friends!"

As the crowd again cheered, Mayor Flynn joined Emma and Jose on stage. "For the second time in one week, I'm honored to share the stage with two awesome kids who are making a difference in our community. Yet I don't just applaud them; I applaud each and every one of you who joined this Stop the Bullying: Rally in the Park. Your presence here gives me great hope. You kids are the key to our future."

Ironically at that point, alerts on several cell phones started ringing. The nasty texts had started. To Emma and Jose's great delight, they did not generate the reaction that General Aveel expected. Kids at the rally enjoyed making a big deal about deleting the texts. Jose and his impromptu band kicked off another round of songs, and the grassy area in front of the stage turned into a dance floor.

Meanwhile Sherpa, wearing big sunglasses and a floppy hat, was keeping a low profile. Even though John and Amanda should be busy hosting their texting party, she did not want to risk their showing up and finding her. "I have no desire to become a prisoner again," she thought grimly. Being tied to a chair for two days not knowing if or when she would be killed had been a chilling experience. Besides, her lip had finally healed, and she really did not want to start biting it again.

Sherpa's mouth watered at the thought of an ice-cream sandwich, so she leisurely strolled toward the vendor with the red cart. He was tall and had curly, blackish-gray hair peeking out underneath his white, pointy hat. He was a popular figure, calling many kids and parents by name; his brown eyes sparkled as he joked around while passing out popcorn and popsicles. Something about him seemed familiar. "Did he look at me funny when handing back my change?" she wondered while walking away from the cart. She dismissed the thought. "No, don't be silly. There is no way he'd know someone from 2310. I've been in spy mode way too long."

Focusing on her treat, Sherpa happily licked the sides of her ice-cream sandwich as she sat underneath a large oak tree. After every bite was gone, she took a peek at the RTD. What she saw took her breath away. Not only was the entire park filled with dazzling white light, but the same white light surrounded each attendee. The best part was that the light started branching out of the park, down the street, and around the local businesses. Adults and teenagers not associated with the rally walked slowly toward the park, curious to see what was going on. The laughter and dancing were contagious!

Sherpa thought humbly, "This is what my mom was trying to tell me. The chancellor of positivity must be a guide to help others recognize the need for good decisions and a positive attitude in order to have a happy life. There is no way I could have orchestrated this rally. Emma and Jose were absolutely *the* chosen ones to help Pineville. There is a lot more to the position than just the title, and it takes more than just being smart. Even if Mom decides not to appoint me chancellor of positivity, I really get it. I can make a difference!"

Just then a familiar voice slammed into her head like hammer. It was John.

"Nice attempt trying to jam our circuits, but you didn't turn the frequencies high enough." John grabbed the RTD out of Sherpa's hand. "Once we download all the data from your time travel device, not only will General Aveel achieve world domination in 2310, but he will control all of history! I will take you to Aveel, but it will be your last trip. Now that we have your device, you are expendable."

"Don't touch me, you hunk of junk," Sherpa yelled as she pulled away from his grasp. There was no way she was going to be taken hostage again.

In the meantime, Jose and the band took a break, but the dance music continued courtesy of his MP3 player. Jose and Emma walked through the crowd toward the red cart to get some ice cream. They happened to notice toward the back end of the park a floppy hat fall off a girl being pushed by a redheaded kid. Instantly they recognized the black curls and broke into a run. "Sherpa!"

"Dude, what's going on?" a panting Jose asked once he and Emma reached them. "Did you get tired of texting?"

"Jose, this is none of your business. If you know what's good for you, you'll get out of here now," John snapped. "Otherwise you can join your friend here at my dad's house."

"You mean General Aveel's house, you moron!" spat out an angry Emma.

"I suspected that the two of you rescued Sherpa from the basement. Now all three of you need to come with me."

Sherpa and Emma looked at each other and then at the RTD in John's right hand. Sherpa gave John a hard push in his chest, catching him off guard. The RTD was jolted out of his hand and into the grass, where Emma quickly scooped it up. Emma activated it and planned to hop the three of them out of the park, but as luck would have it, she didn't need to. The spy in General Aveel's Laboratory must have changed the circuitry in the HuBots. John had a white glow! Just in the nick of time!

Without saying another word, John suddenly turned around and started walking away.

Sherpa jumped up and down. "We did it! Look at the RTD!" Jose and Emma had the same breathtaking moment Sherpa experienced; the white light had spread throughout all of Pineville! "Aveel will never be successful in permanently spreading negativity in this town. We can only hope he returns to 2310 and doesn't try Operation World Domination anywhere else."

Chapter

26

2310 Grand Tour

THAT NIGHT SHERPA USED THE BACK OF her earring and activated the RTD phone to contact Dr. Lichtenstein. The purpose was to relay the good news that Aveel had been defeated and the majority of the Pineville kids had stopped bullying. But they ended up talking for hours about everything, including her assignment to save the future, Dr. L's latest surfing competition, which one of them could run the longer distance…and they ended up discussing the excitement over the Flying Football Championship Series. Before saying good-bye, she asked a special favor.

The next afternoon while Sherpa was waiting in Emma's bedroom for her to return from school, she dictated into the RTD. "Wow, what a whirlwind of a week. No wonder I'm pooped out. When this whole adventure began back in 2310, Dr. L told me to 'ride the wave.' It was a heck of a wave! Mom was right. I never could have learned this much by demanding that people be positive. I had to experience it and learn firsthand from Emma and Jose. There is something about Emma that I can't quite put my finger on—"

As if on cue, the bedroom door opened, and Emma happily leaped onto the pink bedspread and began to excitedly describe the events that had transpired at school. "The principal, Mr. Golya, called Jose and me to his office this morning. He wanted to congratulate us on the Stop the Bullying: Rally in the Park and told us we would get extra credit points in civics class. Mr. Golya also asked us to develop a new club at school to help kids focus on being positive and make good decisions. He thinks that will help kids deal with future bullying attempts." The girls squealed with excitement.

"Congratulations, Emma. Doing the right thing will always be rewarded in some way, somehow, even if you don't know what that is right away. So what are you and Jose going to call this new club?"

Eyes twinkling, Emma said, "SherpaKids. We are going to use the Road of Life to show that the time to have fun being a kid is really short. I wish we could walk down your real Road of Life, but we will have to make do with paper and markers."

Happy tears streamed down Sherpa's face. Her voice breaking a bit, she said, "Aww! Honestly, that means more to me than if my mom does appoint me chancellor of positivity. You and Jose are amazing. I don't think that I could be any prouder of you both! I need for you and Jose to do me one more favor: both of you need to ask your parents if you could spend Saturday with a friend." She added with a mysterious smile, "I have something special planned for you."

With permission granted, on Saturday morning Sherpa activated the RTD and hopped the three of them to the year 2310. They landed in the two-hundredth-floor apartment and were met by Dr. Lichtenstein and Lillian. Jose fist bumped Dr. L, who did not quite understand what Jose was doing.

Lillian hugged Sherpa. "Sweetie, you are home! I missed you so much!"

When Lillian finally released her daughter, Sherpa wiped away a tear and turned toward Dr. L. They gazed into each other's eyes before he enveloped her into his muscular arms. "Dr. Lichtenstein, I assume you don't have a girlfriend?" Sherpa whispered hopefully into his ear.

"I do now—well, that is if she isn't too tired from saving the world," he said, squeezing her tight. "And please call me Troy."

"See," Emma leaned toward Jose, whispering loudly, "I told you he liked her."

Lillian's throat-clearing "Eh-em" caused the couple to reluctantly release their embrace. Attempting to regain her composure, Sherpa said, "Emma and Jose, today is all about thanking you for your role in saving our future. You are going to get a grand tour of the year 2310."

Lillian grinned and asked, "Who wants to start the day by riding in a transport? I have Captain Gabe standing by to fly the fastest one in the fleet. He's waiting for you."

As the group walked out onto the balcony, the look on Jose's face was priceless; he couldn't have been happier if he had been invited to play Carnegie Hall. As he and Emma climbed aboard, Jose turned and asked, "Sherpa, are you coming?"

She shook her head. "No, but Captain Gabe is my favorite pilot of all time. I bet he'll let you take control of the steer stick for a little while."

After Emma and Jose blasted off, Sherpa spent a moment savoring the views of the mountains and the ocean before joining her mother and Dr. L back inside the apartment. The robot poured hot chocolate and delivered Sherpa's much-missed communicator on top of a pink satin pillow.

She hugged her communicator. "I can't wait to talk to Amy. But first things first. Catch me up on what's going on," Sherpa eagerly demanded.

Lillian started. "James at the Intelligence Agency was able to confirm that Alphoneous and his two HuBots left Pineville shortly after the Rally and returned to 2310. After disabling all the HuBot circuitry in Aveel's Laboratory, our spy, Dr. Andy Chou, returned to our Technology Lab and brought with him all of Aveel's data. This will help us tremendously in the future if Alphoneous makes another attempt at Operation World Domination."

"That is great news! It will be a huge relief to everyone at Pineville Middle School not to have John and Amanda there anymore."

"Speaking of Emma and Jose…" said Dr. L hesitantly, "you do remember the failsafe built into the RTD functionality? After they return this afternoon to 2013, they won't remember you anymore."

Sherpa was crestfallen. "I know. I am sad about that, but I will certainly remember them." Forcing a smile, she added, "At least we have this last day to have a ton of fun together with no fears of being taken prisoner by HuBots."

A short time later, the transport silently returned to the balcony, and Emma emerged through the doorway looking ecstatic. "Awesome! We flew clear to the edge of space! It was so close that I felt that I could touch the stars! Then Captain Gabe flew us right next to the skyscrapers and around the entire city. It's beautiful! I so totally want to live here!"

Jose added excitedly, "I got to drive—I mean fly—using the steer stick! Well, only in the open airspace, not around the skyscrapers. And to think I won't be able to drive cars back in 2013 for another 4.5 years."

Sherpa grinned; their excitement was contagious. "Ready for a fast-paced tour of the city?" Being a former tour guide, Sherpa was well versed in showing the highlights of the capital. The group watched part of a flying football game, experimented with the latest communicator, and walked around the spectacular Western World Government offices. Emma in particular was fascinated by Lillian's accomplishments and gushed, "Sherpa, your mom is incredible!"

By the time the group returned to the apartment, Emma and Jose were on cloud nine. It was almost over the top when they saw that lunch had been prepared and delivered by robots. Jose begged to take one home with him.

The last stop on the 2310 grand tour was the Technology Lab. Sherpa laughed, sympathetically of course, when Emma and Jose experienced the sense of impending horror when it appeared the transport would collide into the mountainside. They immediately forgave her, though, upon entering the large doorway and seeing the sights, sounds, and bustling activity of the Technology Lab.

Donning his white lab coat, Dr. L took great pleasure in giving the grand tour, including showing off the super-secret stuff. Emma and Jose interacted with Jackie, the fashion HuBot. Jackie loved Jose's outfit but made a snarky comment about Emma's rumpled shirt.

After a couple hours, Lillian motioned to the timekeeping system on the wall. "I'm sorry to say that it's time to return Emma and Jose to 2013 before their parents start to worry."

Emma and Jose naturally protested but stopped when Sherpa kindly said, "Mom's right, guys. We can't mess around with time travel."

Emma looked up at Sherpa, her blue eyes brimming with tears. "You aren't coming back with us are you…" she said quietly.

"No, I'm not." Sherpa said, emotion overtaking her as she fiercely hugged Emma. "I will miss you both so much. You saved my life, you saved your town from bullies, and most importantly, you saved the world in 2310 by ensuring the End of all Wars treaty wasn't stopped by General Aveel. I've said it before, and I'll say it again: you are heroes! With the SherpaKids Club, please keep helping kids understand why good decisions and positive thinking are so important. It's the future!"

Adding some humor to the moment, Jose struck his spy pose. "Just call me Ramirez, Jose Ramirez. I like my lemonade shaken, not stirred."

Sherpa laughed at the confused looks on the faces of her mother and Dr. L. "I'll explain later."

It was Lillian's turn to hug the kids. Emma held on an extra moment and whispered in her ear, "So are you going to make Sherpa the chancellor of positivity?"

Lillian winked and whispered back, "Yes!"

In the meantime, Jose was sizing up Dr. L. "I know dudes don't talk about this stuff, but you had better be good to Sherpa, or I'll figure out how to get back to 2310 and kick your butt!"

"No worries, Jose. Sherpa is awesome. I will be good to her, I promise," Dr. L replied, crossing his arms and bowing to Jose in Western World fashion. "All right, it's time for the RTD to do its thing."

Dr. Lichtenstein said, "Hold hands and get ready to return to 2013." He shot Jose a look. "Just do it, Jose."

Emma broke away to hug Sherpa one last time. "Thank you for everything and for believing in us. I'll never forget you."

Sherpa's heart ached knowing in ten seconds, Emma wouldn't remember her.

Emma returned to Jose's side, and in a flash, they were gone.

On the transport back to the capital, Lillian noticed Sherpa was uncharacteristically quiet. Taking her daughter's hand, she said, "Sweetheart, this may be difficult to understand, but a wise woman once told me that people come into your life for a reason or a lifetime. Emma and Jose clearly had a purpose—a reason—for you to find them. While you may not have the opportunity to be with them for a lifetime, the impact they made was tremendous. I know you'll never forget them."

Sherpa nodded. "You're right, I will never forget them. I hope they continue to be successful." A light bulb went off in her head, and she perked up. "We can actually find out by looking in the History Archives!" She grabbed her communicator to start researching, but her mom interrupted her.

"Don't just look in the History Archives, but in our own family tree," Lillian said mysteriously.

"Huh?" was the only response that Sherpa could think of.

"Dr. Lichtenstein could not figure out why Emma was able to activate the RTD when it was designed solely for you. So his team did some research and found out some interesting information. Emma is an identical match to a portion of your DNA double helix, which can only mean one thing." Lillian paused for effect.

"What? What does it mean?" Sherpa impatiently yelled out.

With great flourish, Lillian said, "Emma is your great, great, great, great, great, great, great, great, great, great, great, grandmother!"

"Ohmigosh! No wonder I felt so close to her. Mom, did you notice we had the same color eyes?"

"I did indeed. I learned that the flecks of purple in your blue eyes are caused by a recessive gene that skips generations; my grandmother had the same eyes. Your curly hair, though, came from your dad's side of the family. I already did a bit of checking into our family tree. Emma accomplished some great things in her lifetime. I like to think some of that was, in part, thanks to the guidance provided to her at age 11.5 by her great, great, great, great, great, great, great, great, great, great, great, granddaughter."

Sherpa paused a moment to let all the news sink in. "I wish Dad were here—he'd love this!"

"I agree, and between us, I'm starting to have real hope that one day he will come home." Lillian's eyes lit up as she relayed the news. "James has come up with some leads…."

Chapter 27

Back in Pineville

EMMA FOUND HERSELF LOUNGING ON THE couch in Jose's basement while Jose was sitting at his keyboard.

"Jose! Ohmigosh! Wasn't that amazing?" Emma asked excitedly.

"You mean my adaptation of Beethoven's Fifth? It is pretty cool."

"No, I mean yes, your music is great, but duh, I'm talking about the trip to 2310. Remember? Our ride on the transport, the Technology Lab—"

"What are you talking about, Emma? Abuela would say you are going loco. That must have been quite a dream you had during your nap. By the way, you snore." He laughed, then stood up and walked toward the steps. "Saturday Game Night starts in a half hour. I need to get Scrabble and Monopoly set up."

He stuck his head back around the corner. "Oh, don't forget, we need to spend some time tomorrow planning for the first SherpaKids meeting next Monday after school. That was a brilliant idea you had about naming the club after the guides who help hikers climb up Mount Everest. I have some ideas for the Road of Life too. What do you think of putting stars around the room with ages on them? It may be a good visual show that there isn't much time for a kid to be a kid. Oh, and we need a manual too; it helps to have stuff written down."

As Jose left the room, Emma put her head in her hands and said aloud, "It couldn't have been a dream. How could a dream seem so real? I learned so much…" Just then, something shiny on the floor caught her eye. Emma reached down and picked up in her fingertips a small pile of sparkles. She grinned. Next to the sparkles, partially hidden under the couch…was a small, purple-and-gold purse.

The End

Authors Note: Many characters mentioned in this story are real, and you can learn more about them by reading the brief biographies in back of this book, or better yet, check out a book or two from your local library. While the situations that Sherpa helps them with are complete fiction, everyone faces tough decisions at one point or another. All these characters made real life choices when they were kids that impacted their futures—just like you!

Epilogue

"WE CERTAINLY APPRECIATE YOUR TIME and hope you can help us. My husband, Bernard, was one of your students. He disappeared over sixteen years ago in order to hide something that could be dangerous to the fate of the planet."

Dr. McDermott smiled kindly at Lillian. "Aside from my grandson here, Bernard was the best student I ever had. He was smart yet wise beyond his years. He told me that when the time was right, you would come looking for him, and it would be safe to share this information with you. When Bernard discovered the evil contained in Alphoneous Aveel's hologram, he hid in the woods not far from here for several months. However, he knew that if he stayed too long, Aveel and his wicked band of followers would find him. Bernard and I worked on a rudimentary time travel device in the hope that he and the hologram would be safer in another century."

"Grandpa, you worked on time travel principals and never told me?" Dr. Lichtenstein asked.

An impish look came to Dr. McDermott's eye. "Now Troy, if I had told you everything, you never would have had the satisfaction of doing it yourself. I did give you a few hints along the way; however, you alone came up with the other components of the RTD. I never even thought about using a device to read people's energy and use colors to identify whether they were in trouble. That was real genius," he said proudly.

"Do you know where my dad time traveled to? And is he still there?" Sherpa asked.

"Fortunately, I can answer those questions. Bernard and I perfected time travel enough to get him one way to safety. However, sixteen years ago we did not have the technology that would allow him to return to the present day here. He took the hologram and went back in time to the year 1997."

Sherpa quickly did the math, adding sixteen years to 1997. "So that means that now dad is living in the year 2013!" She paused as another revelation hit her. "My dad is in Pineville, isn't he? That would explain why General Aveel keeps focusing so much attention there."

Dr. McDermott nodded. "You are absolutely right, my dear. Good deductive reasoning. You are intelligent—like both your parents. He is still alive."

Lillian sank back in her chair as tears of relief sprang to her eyes.

"How do you know he is alive?" asked James.

"Actually, the credit for this plan goes to my lovely wife. We knew Bernard was going to have to hide in plain sight, but he would have no formal identification in order to hold a job, as was required in 1997. After all, his birth certificate was signed in the twenty-fourth century. So before he left, we accessed the History Archives for key pieces of information during the years 1997 to 2015, such as which teams would win major sporting events, and which companies would have big increases in their stock prices. This gave him money to live, and the bets and stock trades were recorded in logs or newspapers. All transactions were modest so he would not attract attention; he never won any big lotteries. Mrs. McDermott and I regularly monitored the History Archives for anyone by the name of Mark S. Hemingway."

"Mark S. Hemingway? How did he pick that name?" asked Sherpa.

Lillian smiled knowingly. "I think I can answer that. Bernard loved to read, and his favorite authors were Mark Twain and Ernest Hemingway. My guess for the middle initial S is for his daughter Sherpa—or Dr. Seuss!"

Dr. McDermott added, "We had one more back-up plan. If Bernard ever felt that his position in the past was compromised and he may be discovered by Alphoneous Aveel, he would post an advertisement in the New York Times reading, 'Star Gazer seeking assistance. Call MSH immediately.'"

Dr. L posed the question Sherpa desperately wanted to ask. "Grandpa, have you seen this advertisement?"

Dr. McDermott looked first at Sherpa, then at Lillian. "Yes, this morning, right before Troy called me on the secure communicator."

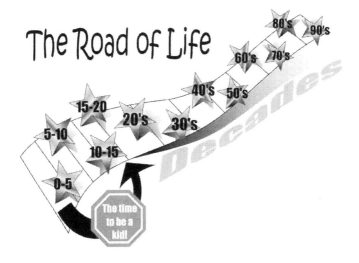

The Road of Life

Sherpa's Manual: How to Fix History and Save the World

Insight #1: Sometimes a straightforward issue just requires providing a minor level of instruction.

<u>What to do:</u>

1. Suggest a specific action.

   ✔ Sir Isaac Newton: "Please go to the apple orchard."

Insight #2: Most people already have the answers inside of them. Sometimes they just need a little help realizing they are really not stuck after all.

<u>What to do:</u>

1. Ask open-ended questions and keep building on those questions. Sometimes questions will "plant a seed" or create a natural path for people to open their minds. Sometimes people just need to talk through an issue.

   ✔ Gustave Eiffel: "What inspires you?"

- ❖ Examples of open-ended questions include:
    - ✔ "What do you like / dislike about ____?"
    - ✔ "How do you feel when ____ happens?"
    - ✔ "What else could you do?"

Insight #2: Ask the Big Question: "Could what you are thinking about doing or not doing hurt yourself or other people?"

  - ✔ Neil Armstrong: "Could you get in trouble, and is it worth it?"

Insight #3: Providing an analogy or similarity helps people relate to a situation.

<u>What to do:</u>

1. Think of an example involving a similar situation
    - ✔ Gustave Eiffel: "If Leonardo Da Vinci could do it, why can't you?"

Insight #4: What works with one person may not work with another.

<u>What to do:</u>

1. Get a feel for each individual and how he or she may best respond—every person and situation is different and will require different questions or methods.

   ✔ Gustave Eiffel—He needed open-ended questions and the comparison to Leonardo Da Vinci.

Insight #5: Never underestimate the importance of encouragement.

   ✔ Amelia Earhart: "Don't let anything stop you from achieving your passion."

   ✔ Peggy Walters: "You can make a difference anywhere!"

Insight #6: Not everyone is open to help or feedback; some people need to find their own way. So you have to respect their choices and just let go.

   ✔ Marilyn Monroe: She so desperately wanted attention that she would do anything to get it.

Insight #7: If you can't change the situation, change your mind-set and how you handle what is going on- control what you can.

<u>What to do:</u>

1. Ask the person how they would act if their life were perfect, and encourage them to act that way now. AKA, "Fake it until you make it!"

   ✔ Oprah Winfrey: You can choose the path you want your life to take.

Insight #8: Some situations can't be fixed with one conversation.

<u>What to do:</u>

1. Be patient and figure out the right time to try again.

   ✔ John Lennon: It took several conversations before he realized that hanging out with the wrong crowd would impact any future success as a musician.

Insight #9: People change all the time—for the better or the worse.

<u>What to do:</u>

   ❖ Don't give up on kids; simply because they are swayed in a certain direction for a period of time, it does not mean they will act that way forever.

- ❖ Share information that helps people make good decisions.

- ❖ Understand that everyone thinks differently and has different life experiences and different goals.

- ❖ Whether we know about it or not, all people have stuff going on in their lives that directly impacts how they act.

- ❖ Be willing to forgive, regain friendships, and move forward.

  - ✔ Amy: As best friends, we were inseparable for years, but for a while, I started hanging with another group of kids and blowing her off. Her feelings were hurt, but she let me know I would always be her friend. After a couple weeks, I apologized, and we were good again.

How to Make Cyber Attacks Worthless

- ❖ Tell your parents or other adults, and most importantly, your friends that it is happening.

- ❖ Reply with surprising remarks or jokes like "Thank you! I agree!"

- ❖ There is power in numbers—make friends with kids who are also getting the texts / emails / IMs.

- ❖ Step in and support kids who are getting bullied- both in person and Cybersupporting.

- ❖ Show confidence- do not let the bullies know that it bothers you.

- ❖ Delete messages without reading- why ruin a good day!

- ❖ When the attack is happening, turn off the cell phones and don't log into email or IM.

- ❖ Know that you are an awesome person and it doesn't matter what bullies think.

- ❖ Report bullying to the school—in writing.

- ❖ Feel sorry for the bullies; they can't be very happy people if they resort to attacking others.

Who's Who? Of Historical Figures (in order of appearance)

Definitions from Wikipedia (www.wikipedia.com)

Sir Isaac Newton (4 January 1643 – 31 March 1727 was

an English physicist, mathematician, astronomer, natural philosopher, alchemist, and theologian who is considered by many scholars and members of the general public to be one of the most influential people in human history. Newton built the first practical reflecting telescope] and developed a theory of color based on the observation that a prism decomposes white light into the many colors that form the visible spectrum.

Edmond Halley (8 November 1656 – 14 January 1742)

was an English astronomer, geophysicist, mathematician, meteorologist, and physicist who is best known for computing the orbit of the eponymous Halley's comet.

Cleopatra VII Philopator (Late 69 BC – August 12, 30

BC) was the last person to rule Egypt as an Egyptian pharaoh – after her death Egypt became a Roman province.

Mohandas Karamchand Gandhi (2 October 1869 – 30

January 1948) was the pre-eminent political and spiritual leader of India during the Indian independence movement. He pioneered *satyagraha*. This is defined as resistance to tyranny through mass civil disobedience, a philosophy firmly founded upon *ahimsa*, or total nonviolence. This concept helped India to gain independence and inspired movements for civil rights and freedom across the world. Gandhi is sometimes referred to as *Mahatma Gandhi* or "Great Soul."

Mother Teresa (26 August 1910 – 5 September 1997),

born **Agnes Gonxha Bojaxhiu** was a Catholic nun of Albanian ethnicity and Indian citizenship who founded the Missionaries of Charity in Calcutta, India, in 1950. For over forty-five years she ministered to the poor, sick, orphaned, and dying, while guiding the Missionaries of Charity's expansion, first throughout India and then in other countries.

Mother Teresa's Missionaries of Charity continued to expand, and at the time of her death, it was operating 610 missions in 123 countries, including hospices and homes for people with HIV/AIDS, leprosy, and tuberculosis; soup kitchens; children's and family counseling programs; orphanages; and schools.

Neil Alden Armstrong (August 5, 1930 – August 25,  2012) was an American astronaut and the first person to walk on the Moon. He was also an aerospace engineer, naval aviator, test pilot, and university professor. Before becoming an astronaut, Armstrong was an officer in the U.S. Navy and served in the Korean War. A participant in the U.S. Air Force's Man in Space Soonest and X-20 Dyna-Soar human spaceflight programs, Armstrong joined the NASA Astronaut Corps in 1962. He made his first space flight, as command pilot of Gemini 8, in 1966, becoming NASA's first civilian astronaut to fly in space. On this mission, he performed the first docking of two spacecraft, with pilot David Scott. Armstrong's second and last spaceflight was as mission commander of the _Apollo 11_ moon landing, in July 1969. On this mission, Armstrong and Buzz Aldrin descended to the lunar surface and spent two and a half hours exploring, while Michael Collins remained in lunar orbit in the Command Module.

Alexandre Gustave Eiffel né **Bönickhausen** (December  15, 1832 – December 27, 1923) was a French structural engineer from the École Centrale Paris, an entrepreneur, and a specialist of metallic structures. He is acclaimed for designing the world-famous Eiffel Tower, built 1887–1889 for the 1889 Universal Exposition in Paris, France. Notable among his other works is the armature for the Statue of Liberty, New York Harbor, United States.

Harriet Tubman (born **Araminta Ross**; c. 1820 or 1821  – March 10, 1913) was an African-American abolitionist, humanitarian, and Union spy during the American Civil War. After escaping from slavery, into which she was born, she made thirteen missions to rescue more than seventy slaves using the network of antislavery activists and safe houses known as the Underground Railroad. She later helped John Brown recruit men for his raid on Harpers Ferry, and in the post-war era struggled for women's suffrage.

Amelia Mary Earhart (born July 24, 1897; missing July

2, 1937; declared legally dead January 5, 1939) was a noted American aviation pioneer and author. Earhart was the first woman to receive the Distinguished Flying Cross, awarded for becoming the first aviatrix to fly solo across the Atlantic Ocean. Earhart joined the faculty of the world-famous Purdue University aviation department in 1935 as a visiting faculty member to counsel women on careers and help inspire others with her love for aviation. She was also a member of the National Woman's Party and an early supporter of the Equal Rights Amendment.

During an attempt to make a circumnavigational flight of the globe in 1937 in a Purdue-funded Lockheed Model 10 Electra, Earhart disappeared over the central Pacific Ocean near Howland Island. Fascination with her life, career, and disappearance continues to this day.

Marilyn Monroe (June 1, 1926 – August 5, 1962), born **Norma Jeane Mortenson**, but baptized **Norma Jeane Baker**,

was an American actress, singer and model. In 1999, Monroe was ranked as the sixth greatest female star of all time by the American Film Institute. In the years and decades following her death, Monroe has often been cited as a pop and cultural icon.

Peggy Walters (no photograph available). The midwife who delivered Abraham Lincoln on February 12, 1809.

Abraham Lincoln (February 12, 1809 – April 15, 1865)  served as the sixteenth President of the United States from March 1861 until his assassination in April 1865. He successfully led the country through its greatest internal crisis, the American Civil War, preserving the Union, ending slavery, and rededicating the nation to nationalism, equal rights, liberty, and democracy. Reared in a poor family on the western frontier, he was mostly self-educated and became a country lawyer, an Illinois state legislator, and a one-term member of the United States House of Representatives, but failed in two attempts at a seat in the United States Senate.

Samuel Langhorne Clemens (November 30, 1835 – April 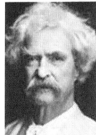 21, 1910), better known by his pen name **Mark Twain**, was an American author and humorist. He is most noted for his novels, *The Adventures of Tom Sawyer* (1876) and its sequel, *Adventures of Huckleberry Finn* (1885), the latter often called "the Great American Novel."

William Shakespeare (baptized 26 April 1564; died 23

April 1616) was an English poet and playwright, widely regarded as the greatest writer in the English language and the world's pre-eminent dramatist. He is often called England's national poet and the "Bard of Avon". His surviving works, including some collaborations, consist of about thirty-eight plays, 154 sonnets, two long narrative poems, and several other poems. His plays have been translated into every major living language and are performed more often than those of any other playwright.

Elvis Aaron Presley (January 8, 1935 – August 16, 1977) was

one of the most popular American singers of the twentieth century. A cultural icon, he is widely known by the single name **Elvis**. He is often referred to as the "King of Rock and Roll" or simply "the King."
Prescription drug abuse severely compromised his health, and he died suddenly in 1977 at the age of forty-two. Presley is regarded as one of the most important figures of twentieth-century popular culture. He had a versatile voice and unusually wide success encompassing many genres, including country, pop ballads, gospel, and blues. He is the best-selling solo artist in the history of popular music. Nominated for fourteen competitive Grammys, he won three, and received the Grammy Lifetime Achievement Award at age thirty-six. He has been inducted into four music halls of fame.

The Beatles were an English rock band, formed in Liverpool in 1960, and one of the most commercially successful and

critically acclaimed acts in the history of popular music. From 1962 the group consisted of John Lennon (rhythm guitar, vocals), Paul McCartney (bass guitar, vocals), George Harrison (lead guitar, vocals) and Ringo Starr (drums, vocals). Rooted in skiffle and 1950s rock and roll, the group later worked in many genres ranging from pop ballads to psychedelic rock, often incorporating classical and other elements in innovative ways. The nature of their enormous popularity, which first emerged as the "Beatlemania" fad, transformed as their songwriting grew in sophistication. The group came to be perceived as the embodiment of progressive ideals, seeing their influence extend into the social and cultural revolutions of the 1960s.

William Clark Gable (February 1, 1901 – November 16, 1960), known as **Clark Gable**, was an American film actor

most famous for his role as Rhett Butler in the 1939 Civil War epic film _Gone with the Wind_, in which he starred with Vivien Leigh. In 1999, the American Film Institute named Gable seventh among the greatest male stars of all time. He was nicknamed "The King of Hollywood."

Mount Everest (Tibetan: ཇོ་མོ་གླང་མ, **Chomolungma** or **Qomolangma** /ˈtʃoʊmoʊˌlɑːŋmə/ *CHOH-moh-LAHNG-mə*,[6][7] *"Holy Mother"*; Chinese: 珠穆朗玛峰; pinyin: *Zhūmùlǎngmǎ Fēng*; Nepali: सगरमाथा, **Sagarmāthā**) is the Earth's highest mountain, with a peak at 8,848 meters (29,029 ft) above sea level. It is located in the Mahalangur section of the Himalayas. The international border between China and Nepal runs across the precise summit point

Joseph John Rosenthal (October 9, 1911 – August 20, 2006)

was an American photographer who received the Pulitzer Prize for his iconic World War II photograph *Raising the Flag on Iwo Jima*, taken during the Battle of Iwo Jima. His picture became one of the best-known photographs of the war.

Henry Ford (July 30, 1863 – April 7, 1947) was an

American industrialist, the founder of the Ford Motor Company, and sponsor of the development of the assembly line technique of mass production. His introduction of the Model T automobile revolutionized transportation and American industry.

Wolfgang Amadeus Mozart (27 January 1756 – 5 December

1791), was a prolific and influential composer of the Classical era. He composed over six hundred works, many acknowledged as pinnacles of symphonic, concertante, chamber, piano, operatic, and choral music. He is among the most enduringly popular of classical composers.

Johann Sebastian Bach (31 March 1685 [O.S. 21 March] –

28 July 1750) was a German composer, organist, harpsichordist, violist, and violinist whose ecclesiastical and secular works for choir, orchestra, and solo instruments drew together the strands of the Baroque period and brought it to its ultimate maturity

Ludwig van Beethoven (baptized 17 December 1770 – 26

March 1827) was a German composer and pianist. He is considered to have been the most crucial figure in the transitional period between the Classical and Romantic eras in Western classical music and remains one of the most famous and influential composers of all time. His hearing began to deteriorate

in the late 1790s, yet he continued to compose, conduct, and perform, even after becoming completely deaf.

Tutankhamun (1341 BC – 1323 BC) was an Egyptian pharaoh

of the eighteenth dynasty during the period of Egyptian history known as the New Kingdom. The 1922 discovery by Howard Carter of Tutankhamun's nearly intact tomb received worldwide press coverage. It sparked a renewed public interest in ancient Egypt, for which Tutankhamun's burial mask remains the popular symbol. Exhibits of artifacts from his tomb have toured the world.

Marie Skłodowska Curie (7 November 1867 – 4 July

1934) was a physicist and chemist of Polish upbringing and subsequent French citizenship. She was a pioneer in the field of radioactivity and the first person honored with two Nobel Prizes—in physics and chemistry. She was also the first female professor at the University of Paris.

George Washington (February 22, 1732 – December 14,

1799) was the dominant military and political leader of the new United States of America from 1775–1797, leading the American victory over Britain in the American Revolutionary War as commander in chief of the Continental Army, 1775–1783, and presiding over the writing of the Constitution in 1787. As the unanimous choice to serve as the first president of the United States (1789–1797), he developed the forms and rituals of government that have been used ever since and built a strong, well-financed national government that avoided war, suppressed rebellion, and won acceptance among Americans of all types. Acclaimed ever since as the "Father of his country," Washington, along with Abraham Lincoln (1809–1865), has become a central icon of republican values, self sacrifice in the name of the nation, American nationalism, and the ideal union of civic and military leadership.

Elizabeth I (7 September 1533 – 24 March 1603) was Queen

regnant of England and Queen regnant of Ireland from 17 November 1558 until her death. Sometimes called **The Virgin Queen**, **Gloriana**, or **Good Queen Bess**, Elizabeth was the fifth and last monarch of the Tudor dynasty.

Pocahontas (c. 1595 – March 21, 1617), later known as

Rebecca Rolfe, was a Virginia Indian chief's daughter notable for having assisted colonial settlers at Jamestown. She converted to Christianity and married the English settler John Rolfe. After they traveled to London, she became famous in the last year of her life.

The **Berlin Wall** (German: *Berliner Mauer*) was a barrier

constructed by the German Democratic Republic (GDR, East Germany) starting August 13, 1961, that completely cut off West Berlin from surrounding East Germany and from East Berlin. The barrier included guard towers placed along large concrete walls, which circumscribed a wide area (later known as the "death strip") that contained anti-vehicle trenches, "fakir beds," and other defenses. The Soviet-dominated Eastern Bloc officially claimed that the wall was erected to protect its population from fascist elements conspiring to prevent the "will of the people" in building a Socialist State in East Germany. However, in practice, the Wall served to prevent the massive emigration and defection that marked Germany and the communist Eastern Bloc during the post-World War II period.

The fall of the Berlin Wall paved the way for German reunification, which was formally concluded on October 3, 1990.

Charles Rozell "Chuck" Swindoll (born October 18, 1934)

is an evangelical Christian pastor, author, educator, and radio preacher.

Oprah Winfrey (born **Orpah Gail Winfrey**; January 29, 1954)

is an American media proprietor, talk show host, actress, producer, and philanthropist. Winfrey is best known for her self-titled, multi-award-winning talk show, which has become the highest-rated program of its kind in history and was nationally syndicated from 1986 to 2011. She has been ranked the richest African-American of the 20th century, the greatest black philanthropist in American history, and was for a time the world's only black billionaire. She is also, according to some assessments, the most influential woman in the world.

About the Author:

A believer of being part of something bigger than herself, Lori Costew is passionate about kids and the positive impact they can have on the world—if they choose to do so. Born a Buckeye, she currently lives in Northville, Michigan, with her husband and two young children. Like Sherpa, Lori loves all things chocolate and her favorite place is on the beach with sand in her toes!

Made in the USA
Charleston, SC
15 February 2013